Arise Gile
9th Heavenly Cat

Other Dank House Manor titles by author

Jubjub Juice
Byron Beyond the Firmament
Hound of the Biscuit Barrell
Trash Island
iDrip

Other titles by the author published by Weasel
Press / Sinister Stoat

Tales in Liquid Time
Not Kafka
Cause for Concern
Miffed & Peeved in the UK
Taste & See

Arise Giles Bastet
9th Heavenly Cat
by
Neil S. Reddy

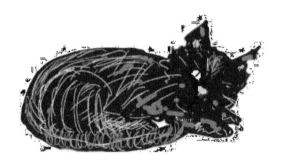

Arise Giles Bastet 9th Heavenly Cat
Neil S. Reddy

ISBN 978-0-9954753-9-7

Dank House Manor Publications 2024

ACKNOWLEDGMENTS
Extracts previously published by Sinister Stoat USA, and by Dank House Manor UK.

This is a work of fiction containing historical figures any resemblance to any living person is entirely coincidental.

Thanks to
NATSUME SŌSEKI (夏目 漱石)

Dedicated to
Angeline Morrison
for her album 'The Sorrow Songs.'

&
Raisin, Behemoth, Kodak
&
all the cats that have gone before.

And a special thank you to
Helen Lindley
for her musical & lyrical collaboration & contribution.

A dog is the only being who has seen his god first-hand.
Jack London

In ancient times cats were worshipped as gods; they have not forgotten this.
Terry Pratchett

CONTENTS

AWAKEN GILES BASTET, 9th HEAVENLY CAT

Stephen Gower tore the wooden boarding from the shop's window. He was moving in and had three weeks to get the place ready. Lots to be done. The property had once been a bookshop, but it had been empty for nearly a decade, something Stephen couldn't get his head around, because the shop's location was retail perfect, prime real-estate. Positioned at the centre of the high-street, opposite the zebra crossing, right next to a coffee shop, with a small car park outback, really the perfect setting for any business. The floor space wasn't massive, but it would do him while his business grew. There was even a little office and a watertight cellar for stock – and he got it all for a song, a bloody song. The window was dusty and web encrusted but still intact, and at almost two yards wide it provided a perfect view into the premises; bloody perfect - all he had to do was deal with the old display.

A somewhat raggedy, worn at the edges, loose at the seams, cloth cat, sat in the window. It had obviously been placed there to emulate that cat from the children's television show, the cat with the pink stripes. Stephen couldn't recall the cat's name. He was too young to remember the program, but he'd seen it in one of those nostalgic TV shows about the 'golden age of television.' All he knew was, it was a program about a fat cat that told stories, a charming 'olde worlde' kind of thing - too slow for modern kids, a thing of its time. The children that had ran home to watch the show were now grandparents. Which meant the cat sitting in the window had been there a very long time - and by the look of the thing it had been sitting there for an age before the window was boarded up. Years of sitting in the sun had bleached the colour from its fur, which meant selling it as a collector's item was out of the question. Stephen felt a slight pang, it was a shame - ten years of incarceration, forgotten and gathering dust and now he had to throw it out - better get it over with, get it done and move on.

The door opened with a slight rasp, and Stephen made a mental note to get some WD40. He'd changed the bulbs before seeing to the boardings and was amazed to see the difference daylight made to the shop's interior - even through the caked-on dirt the light made such a difference; the place looked magical. Stephen just knew his business would do well here, he just knew it. He leant into the window display and reached for the cat.

As soon as his fingers touched the fur his hand recoiled. It wasn't that soft artificial stuff he expected to find – it was real fur. There was a dead cat in his window display. Stephen gritted his teeth and lifted the cat from its shroud of dust.

Directly outside the window a schoolboy with a beautifully shaped ice-cream cone, tripped over his own feet and crashed face down onto the pavement. A moment later a pensioner on a large-framed bicycle, drew up to the zebra crossing. Seeing the fallen child, he clipped the curb and spun head over heels onto the pavement, landing directly on top of the schoolboy. Three seconds later, a traffic warden, rushing to give assistance, slid across the spilt ice-cream, fell backwards, and hit his head on the pavement with a bone crunching thwack. This caused a passing guide dog to pull away from its charge and jump into the road. Seeing this, the driver of an aging Renault 19 swerved sharply, clipping the pensioner's fallen bicycle. The bike's front wheel flew up into the air, shot through the plate glass window and knocked Stephen Gower senseless. He came to seconds later; heard the commotion outside the window; and looking out asked; 'Is everybody okay?'

A shard of the ancient plate glass window dropped from its powdered fixings and severed his head. The blood flowed into the street, as the mummified stuffed cat fell from Stephen's twitching hand.

The cat blinked, yawned, and stretched - Giles Bastet, 9th Heavenly Cat, lord high overseer of accidental death, was awake.

GILES BASTET TOWN CAT

A shabby tabby cat with a jagged notch missing from its left ear stared at the sign that proclaimed 'Bekonscot Model Village,' was closed to the public. Of course, being a cat, he couldn't read the sign. But there was something strangely intriguing about the shapes on the board that comforted him. Pleasant memories of better times when he was… something more than just a stray cat – but what and when that was, escaped him. His little head was full of images and shapes that he just couldn't place; it was intriguing, he liked the sensation. He would have to investigate, so much to discover, what a fine thing it was to be alive and curious.

The cat stepped through the twisted bars of the wrought iron gate and sauntered inside. What he found beyond the gates didn't disappoint, a miniature human world frozen in time. It made him feel important. A picture formed in his head of a similar place seen long ago. A miniature world, complete with a mountain called Fuji, with snow on its peak, yes, he remembered the servants replacing the snow first thing every morning, before the Old Emperor came to view his map of the world. And there had been a forest of bonsai trees, and little streams, with tiny bamboo houses; and something else… yes, little mice that ran over the miniature hills like little goats. Goats, he remembered goats, with their funny wrong way round eyes, he liked goats, goats were fun. It was coming back to him, good times, when he'd been something more…but what was it, what was he? Intriguing, he'd keep on looking, the answer was just a whisker away, he could feel it. He brushed purposefully against a red double decker bus, scratched his good ear against the top of the town hall and stared into the town's tiny hotel window and saw a bathtub; now that reminded him of something else – a female human with dark skin and an amusing nose who bathed in milk; what was her name? And where was that? Somewhere hot and somewhere else, far away from the miniature mountain and the old man they called Emperor. Then there was the cold place, colder than the snow the servants put on the mountain called Fuji; and the cry of a child, or was it wolves, ah yes wolves, goats and a talking donkey, he remembered them, good times, sometime. And then there was Paris, and a thing called a ship, what was he doing on a ship? And then there had been the songs, songs sang to him and songs about him…

whoever he was? How very curious it was not to know who he was; he liked it. The cat sat himself down by the church and proceeded to lick his front paw; it felt like it had been a very long time since he'd washed, and he needed to settle himself, gather his thoughts and remember who he was - because he was something important, he was sure of that. His head was full of shapes and images just like the walls in that place where the bald humans brought him and his brothers and sisters milk; yes he had brothers and sisters and a mother, a mighty mother…

A size ten bother-boot shot the cat across the village and into the concrete frontage of the town hall. Another boot, size nine, stamped hard on the cat's pelvis - the crunch made Val and his thugs, Micky and Spat wince; and then laugh like blood hungry hyenas. Who can blame them? Spice makes you do crazy things.

'Did you hear that? Did you hear that? You are one fucked up kittycat. Right royally fucked!' Val jeered at the grey crumpled body.

Micky, a bell-faced no neck block of lard with teeth like knuckles, reached down and grabbed the cat by the tail. Lifting it high above his head he spun it round and round, jeering; 'Look it's so small in here. Hardly room to swing a cat,'

Val and Spat laughed, Micky was such a clown.

'Man, you crack me up Micky, 'ere let me 'ave a go.' The cat was tossed across the village. Val caught it and slammed the ragged thing into the ground, once, twice and then - just for good measure - he bent its back over the roof of the Post Office and elbow dropped the twitching thing.

'Oh, that's got to hurt, got to hurt right, got to hurt.' Spat slathered with excitement.

Val picked up the limp body and gripped it by its throat. Twisting the head around with thumb and forefinger, he intoned the theme from 'Psycho', thinking it the theme from 'The Exorcist.' His idiot pals didn't spot the error and didn't have the balls to correct him if they had. 'Oi Spat, heads!' Val threw the broken carcass overarm to his henchman. The cat spun through the air, twisted head over broken tail.

Spat attempted a header, missed, caught the bloody bundle on his knee, dropped it to his left foot, and kicked it through the town's only pelican crossing; 'Goal!'

'You got any string?' Val laughed.

'What for?'

'I want to string it up, so the old farts and kiddies see it when they come in.'

'Rig it up to the church steeple,' Spat snorted, 'like a sacrifice.'

'Yeah like a sacrifice,' Micky agreed.

'So, you got any?'

'What?'

'String you arse!'

'I've got an old boot lace,' Micky offered, reaching into his bomber-jacket.

'Just the job.'

The lace was wrapped around the cat's limp neck and tied, good and tight, to the church's miniature Norman tower. It looked ghastly, and the lads loved it.

'Something's missing…' Val pondered.

'Yeah…yeah, you're right,' Micky mumbled without a thought in his head.

'We could set fire to it,' Spat suggested.

'How do you turn a cat into a dog?' Val asked but received no answers. 'You cover it with petrol and light it. It goes WOOF!'

'Good one! Woof! Woof!' barked Micky.

'Woof!' barked Spat.

'Right that's enough, nobody's turning me into a dog,' a voice snarled.

'Who said that; who's there…?' The lads turned about, fists clenched, ready to run, ready to fight their way out.

'I know I should thank you really… a kick to the head was just what I needed, but you took it too far. I can't let it go, you understand that; it just wouldn't be right.'

Val, Spat and Micky watched as the cat extricated its broken body from its bonds and stretched itself back into shape on the church's roof.

'Oh shit! You seeing this Val?'

'It's the Spice, it's the Spice!' Val demanded.

'So here it is, I'm a god, Giles Bastet, 9th heavenly cat, lord high overseer of accidental death… and you've pissed me off. You broke my back; rude doesn't even come close, downright disrespectful, some might even say blasphemous.'

'Make it stop Val! Make it stop!'

'It's the Spice mate, the bloody Spice, I'm not havin' it!' Val ran at the cat, swung his boot in hard and connected with nothing but a blue flash of light. He fell backwards into the butcher's shop – which being made from concrete, caved in the back of his head.

Spat instantly ejected the contents of his stomach into Micky's face. Micky reeled away in disgust, fell over 'Annie's Newsagents', and landed face down in Church Street, where the tiny newspaper-boy Eric was forever delivering the morning papers. Eric's miniature cast-iron bicycle tore into Micky's carotid artery. A plume of blood rose and fell across the miniature town, frightening Spat so that he ran from the village, straight into the twisted rungs of the wrought-iron gate. Dazed and blinded by the blood that flowed from his temple, Micky fell to his knees and slumped to the floor; 'please, please, not me,' he pleaded, and then passed out.

Giles Bastet, 9th Heavenly Cat, lord high overseer of accidental death, son of Bastet Goddess of Protection (Blessed be her name), stepped onto Micky's face and settled down to wash. It had been a long time since he'd had a really thorough wash, and he would take his time, he was in no rush, that was one of the joys of being a god, all time was his to play with, he would wait and wash, at least until the gurgling stopped.

STRAY CAT

Listen, Giles Bastet has come unstuck in time. Giles has gone to sleep in a window and awaked in a collection of short stories. Giles' natural divinity has become adulterated by the precise habits and twisted inclinations of poets and writers. Giles asks them how this happened, and they keep telling him; 'how and why are not important, character matters. Character is everything.' Giles has been exposed to the power of man's imagination, and their goofy visions of the world, distorting his passage through time. And so he goes from one disjointed incident to another. A ball of cuteness, rubbing his head against the world, inflicting terrible consequences on all he touches, ending empires and ending lives.

This is a story about Giles Bastet. I can't tell you how long this ridiculous attempt to create an amusing analogy of chance has taken me. Or how crushing it is to discover its utterly dependent on a feline protagonist, and a god at that. I have had some very bad experiences with deities and their followers. Giles informs me that everybody has, and I shouldn't take it to heart. But that's easy for him to say, he's a cat and a deity to boot. I tell him that I am the author of his divinity and his cuteness. And Giles insists he is the author of my doom; I suspect he may be right.

He says, 'this is a terrible book you're writing.'

I say, 'what do you know, you're a cat.'

He says, 'I've spent time with Byron, Blume, Burroughs, Capote, Colette, Cortázar, Dahl, Defoe, Dickens, Duffy…'

I tell him to, 'stop naming writers alphabetically.'

'…Hemingway, Highsmith, Joyce, Le Guin, Perec, Poe, Vonnegut and Woolf.'

'And you can leave-off dropping the big names too. And anyway, when did all this literary carousing occur?' I ask.

'When isn't important; character is everything.'

'You've got it bad Giles. But tell me, how did you fall into this literary rabbit hole?'

'How is not…'

'Pack it in Giles!'

And off he goes.

Two poets, a young couple, one English, the other American; were returning to their cramped London house in Charlotte Square, when they came across a bedraggled, sickly looking tabby cat with a ragged ear, sitting at the side of the road. It looked as if someone had beaten it up. They couldn't just ignore it, they were poets and poets can't ignore anything, except bills and other people's feelings. The Englishman wanted to take it home, the American insisted he take it to the nearest veterinarian. The American won and Giles spent the next week locked in a cage. Unfortunately, the young poets had busy complicated personal lives, so forgot to check on the stray cat's progress. At the end of three weeks, with no claims made for the tabby cat, the vet, Dr Simon Jacobs - he had the right to the professional title and made sure everyone used it - decided that London did not need another stray unwanted tomcat; and drew-up a dose of sodium pentobarbital. He administered the standard lethal dose carefully to the cat's front right leg; took a hit from the vodka bottle in his top draw, a salute to the cat's passing, and then took another, as reward for a job well done.

The body was placed in a chest freezer at the back of the property to await collection. The next day, when Eugene Falks, crematorium technician, arrived to collect the weekly load, he was alarmed and somewhat unsettled to hear an ardent mewling coming from the chest freezer. He opened the lid, and there was a frosty looking tabby staring at him with large baneful eyes. Eugene immediately alerted the vet's receptionist. The receptionist alerted Maud Standling, a veterinarian nurse of ten years standing, who removed the cat from the freezer, and assured Eugene she would make Dr Jacobs aware of this egregious oversight, and that it would never happen again. When Maud informed Dr Simon Jacobs of the situation, she was not gentle; strident might be the best way of describing the talking-to Jacob's endured. Maud had standards, the surgery had standards, and a reputation, a duty of care! Other mistakes had been made, she'd tried to protect him, made excuses for him, but this was going too far! What would happen if news got out of such a thing happening? Dr Jacobs was chastened by Maud's words, looked guiltily to his desk drawer, and promised it would never happen again. The cat was given a full medical, a bowl of best quality cat food and a bed (cage) for the night. But seventy-two hours later, no owner could be found for the moggy, so Simon took a hit from the bottle in his desk drawer and administered another lethal injection. He then checked the cat's vital signs twice and carried the body to the freezer himself; and then treated himself to another shot from the desk drawer. Later that same day, Maud was passing the chest freezer, when she heard a forlorn mewing. Maud investigated; retrieved the cat and with a stern accusatory stare, presented the cat to Simon. Simon was baffled, bewildered, and deeply embarrassed. Maud informed Simon that she knew all about the bottle of vodka he kept in his drawer and that she was a breath away from reporting him to the Royal College and having him struck off. Simon laid his heart on the table for Maud. Whatever had happened to this cat was nothing to do with his drinking; he had given the cat the correct dose, administered in the correct fashion and the cat had most definitely been dead when he placed it in the freezer. He had no reasonable explanation for the cat's resurrection, but he would check with their medical supplier, and his colleagues to make sure there had been no other incidents and it would never, ever happen again. Maud was not convinced; so Simon also agreed to talk to his GP about his drinking, and to refrain from euthanising, unless Maud was there to supervise. The cat was immediately fed, wrapped in a warm blanket, and placed in the nicest cage the surgery had to offer. Simon double checked his stock of sodium pentobarbital, called his supplier, and enquired if there had been any other incidents that might suggest there was a bad batch in circulation. There had not. Simon helped himself to a double shot from his draw and brooded; who the hell was this nurse to boss him around – and who the hell was this cat to ruin his reputation.

Simon stayed late at the surgery, telling Maud there were accounts he needed to finish. Maud didn't find this difficult to believe. And as soon as Maud and the other staff were out of the way, Simon helped himself to a double, double shot from the draw, collected the cat from the nicest cage they had in the surgery, placed it on the clinic table, and drew-up a dose of sodium pentobarbital. He administered it to the cat's neck. The cat keeled over. Simon double checked the vital signs and sat back with his bottle to watch. For two hours, nothing happened, the cat was dead. Just after midnight Simon did a quick round of the cages, checking his charges were as comfortable as possible and progressing nicely; all was well. And then returned to the clinic; the cat was sitting up on the table looking at him with accusing eyes. Simon emptied the bottle, drew-up a doubly lethal dose, sank the needle into the cat's haunches, watched it fall, turned to dispose of the used needle; but when he turned back, the cat was preening itself on his clinic table. Simon's exclamation of drunken rage woke all his overnight charges. Ignoring the howls and cries of distress emanating from the cages, Simon filled three large syringes. One with sodium pentobarbital, one with ketamine, and one with bleach – nothing and no-one could withstand such a pharmaceutical onslaught.

The first syringe stopped the cat's heart, the contents of the second syringe was then administered with a long needle straight into the cat's heart. A wide bore needle was then driven through the cat's skull directly into the cat's brain; just to be on the safe side.

Simon felt strangely aroused by the experience. Did he in fact enjoy killing animals? And why had he denied himself the freedom of such an insight for so long? Simon felt free, elated and empowered and… and then he heard the cat meow. There it was looking at him; mocking him. The bastard even purred. Enraged, Simon grabbed a scalpel from his draw and rushed at the cat. He took hold of its head and slashed wildly at the creature's neck – which along with the rest of the animal disappeared in a blue flash – causing Simon's scalpel to pass through his wrist in a deep wide arc. Simon saw his wrist, red and pumping, turned about looking for the cat, saw the blood pouring out across the floor, heard Maud's scornful voice in his head, and fainted.

Dr Simon Jacob's body was discovered the next morning when Eugene Falks came to unload the freezer. Giles Bastet has come unstuck in time, and so he
goes.

PARK LIFE

Giles Bastet, 9th Heavenly Cat, lord high overseer of accidental death, son of Bastet, Goddess of Protection (Blessed be her name), was in a reflective mood. Giles had been through a lot recently, but when and where that recently had occurred was hard to tell. Being an eternal being, detached from the confines of time could be a dislocating experience. He knew he'd been asleep for a long time - relatively speaking - and although when and where wasn't really relevant, why he'd chosen to do such a thing really was; why would he have done such a reckless thing? How were the humans meant to cope without him? His failure to carry out his beatific duties bothered Giles, what was he if he wasn't enacting his divine purpose? This thought bothered him even more. How had he become so reflective? Being 'lord high overseer of accidental death,' meant that the scope of Giles' reflections was limited, and he knew it. How could he, a divine being, be so limited? What he needed to do was to focus his thoughts, and there's only one way a cat can do that; he needed a box. He needed to crawl into a box and indulge in some serious self-reflection. The appropriate box presented itself beside a bus shelter opposite a municipal park. There's nothing like a good box for some serious contemplation; Giles stepped inside, curled himself into a ball and began gathering his thoughts.

Firstly, he considered how fortunate he was in comparison to the many unlucky fates his mortal brothers had encountered over the centuries. Volcanoes, earthquakes and forest fires – sitting on a snake you thought was a branch, all these he had tasted. Then there were the old favourites; falls, drownings, fishbones and furballs that choked you to death. And then there was mankind and all its machinations. The trouble was, once the ape-servants had progressed beyond serving cats food they had begun to spread across the world. And once those dexterous fingers were no-longer busy finding fleas, they had begun to invent and mechanise – it was like a disease with the creatures. Where cats saw a comfortable tree, ideal for sleepy sunning, they saw a table or a catapult – the very name made him shiver. And once the servants had grown in numbers and built city's it seemed as if the variety and complexity of possible deaths had multiplied exponentially. Once they had to worry about being put down wells, now there were cogs, cars, trucks, airtight compartments, poisons and all manner of ways of losing a life. All a cat had to do was fall asleep in the wrong warm place and he could find himself transported across the country, torn to shreds by machinery or cooked to a crisp. And they used to be such good servants, where did it all go wrong? But enough of that; time to focus on Giles, what was Giles about?

The top of the cardboard box sagged as a heavy weight was placed upon it, sealing Giles Bastet inside. A moment later the box shifted and began rocking rapidly from side to side. Giles knew he was being carried, and he knew from eternal experience that whoever was carrying him was running. Whatever was going to happen next? He was curious to find out.

Samuel Pipit located the breach in the park railings and crawled through, pushing a Smiths Crisps cardboard box before him. Once through, he kept low and ran across a small stretch of well-manicured lawn, and into a vigorous clump of rhododendrons. Once within the shelter of their ample leaves, Pipit turned on his pencil-torch and followed a barely discernible track through the bushes that led him into his favourite spot in the park. A small clearing encompassed by five heavily leaved beech trees, an overgrown boxwood hedge, and a mass of brambles so thick it had persuaded the ageing park keeper to designate the pentangle of trees as a 'wild area.'

Pipit placed the box on the floor, sealed it with a sturdy house brick, and then reached deep into the base of the boxwood hedge, and retrieved a wooden broom handle. One end of the handle had been sharpened to a sturdy point, whilst the other had a triangular wooden coat hanger fixed to it with heavy black duct tape. Pipit shuffled around on his knees, feeling the ground with his free hand, until he found the pre prepared hole – into which he drove the sharp end of the homemade gibbet. He then removed a square white envelope from his coat pocket, which he placed beside the brick on top of the cardboard box. Pipit undressed and placed his clothing in a neat pile beside the now meowing box. Once naked he took up the white envelope, and from it produced a filament thin metal guitar string. It shone like a gold circle in the beam of his pencil torch. His reverie was broken by violent scratching from the box. Pipit gave the box a sharp kick and then repositioned the house brick – losing the sacrifice now would be a tragedy. Pipit unwound the guitar string, threaded it's end back through its hollow ball end, to form a perfect noose. Slipping the noose over his right wrist, he clenched the other end firmly between his teeth and knelt by the box. Pipit laid his palm on the box's top and pushed the brick to the floor. Pipit turned-up a corner of the box top, a tabby cat's head immediately appeared in the space he'd created. Pipit grabbed the back of its neck, rendering it helpless, he slipped the noose from his wrist over the cat's head and around its throat. The cat spat and thrashed as the noose was pulled tight, but there was no escaping now. Pipit lifted the hissing, spitting thing from the box by the scruff of its neck. Once clear of the box, Pipit released his grip of the cat's neck and took hold of the guitar string with both hands. The cat writhed like a freshly caught Salmon – a comparison that amused Pipit greatly; 'Looks like I caught myself a cat-fish,' he smirked, 'round and round we go, where we stop, nobody knows.' Pipit swung his prize around three times in a full circle. This done, he carefully wound the free end of the guitar string around the extended corner of the coat hanger. The cat dangled mere inches from the earth. Its wildly swinging tail whipping the ground as its four legs desperately clawed the air.

Pipit pissed on the cat. Raised his arms high and danced around the thrashing thing as he addressed the sky: 'Dark spirits of earth and space hear me. Rise, awake and salute, hale and praise the one true god, Lucifer Bright Morning Star, Unholy King of Dark Fire, God of the Left Hand Path, rightful ruler of all that walks and crawls upon and beneath the Earth. Hear me master, I bring you my pledge, my gift of blood to honour your name,' Pipit picked up the brick and held it defiantly towards the dark night sky, 'Sky God, I defy you! Look down on me and tremble! Lord Lucifer envelop your servant in your scorched wings and accept my pledge of pain and blood.

Pipit swung the brick into the cat's body, again and again, beating the thing to a pulp. Elated and aroused, Pipit threw himself to the ground, filled his cupped hands with the twitching mass' bloody residue, and frantically worked his erect member to a whimpering climax. He rolled onto his back, spent and smeared with gore.

'How was that for you?' Giles Bastet, 9th Heavenly Cat, lord high overseer of accidental death, asked Pipit as he extricated himself from the guitar string noose.

Pipit watched, frozen in horror as the tabby cat reformed itself with a shake and a stretch and then proceeded to sit on his chest.

'I have to say I thought we'd got past all this sacrifice nonsense back in Egypt? I know the Romans indulged but that was more entertainment than holy observance. I suppose the Freemasons have had their advocates over the years, but really that was just a poor reflection of those Nile Delta architects.'

'Did Satan send you?' Pipit croaked.

'No he did not, never heard of him. Look, this is what I said to the High Priest of Egypt. Holy Queen Bastet, blessed be her name, my mother, is a cat, why would she want sacrifices made of her mortal form. It makes no sense. Mice yes, rats with bells on their tails… fantastic! But cats, no, stop killing the cats.'

Pipit slapped the talking cat from his chest and jumped to his feet. As he turned to run his right foot collided with the fallen brick, breaking his little piggy toe. Stumbling forward his left foot became entangled with the cardboard box. Sliding sideways his shoulder clipped the trunk of a beach tree, which sent him spinning into and over the ill-managed box tree hedge. Landing heavily on his side Pipit felt a rib crack and rolled forward, straight into the thickest mass of the bramble patch.

'Where do you think you're going?' the tabby cat in the tree branch growled at him.

Maddened by panic and the pain of the stinging thorns, Pipit charged through the brambles. Razor toothed thorns bit his legs, slashed his stomach, and tore at his balls and cock – but Pipit made it through. Blooded and screaming he scrambled up the park's iron railings – tearing the inside of his thigh, and puncturing his scrotum. Undeterred he ran blindly on, straight into a lone police officer – who, taken by surprise, proceeded to beat Pipit with his truncheon until the blood covered intruder stopped moving.

Pipit awoke on a hospital bed, parched, his body aching, head swimming with fever. He needed a drink. Bewildered and frightened his unfocused eyes scanned the small room for a glass of water

'Awake at last,' the tabby cat at the end of the bed stated, 'I must say I was impressed by your turn of speed, young man, very impressive. So how you doing? Not too good I think.'

Pipit tried to scream but his mouth wouldn't move. His entire jaw was stiff, set like tanned leather. Pipit gripped his jaw and tried to force his torn fingers between his lips but his jaw would not budge.

'Good to see you being so cheerful. Lovely smile I must say, just the way to face eternity. What would eternity be without a sense of humour ah?' the tabby cat moved slowly to his chest, stepping on every wound and bruise as it did so. Once ensconced the cat opened its legs wide and began to lick itself clean, 'Don't mind me, you just carry on. Cleanliness is everything, wouldn't want to get sepsis would we? So easily done too, the smallest nick or cut, and if you're not very lucky, if you don't get to it in time... you know what? That's odd, how do I know about sepsis? I wonder where I picked up that little gem? The thing is, I've been out of circulation for a while, or not, it's difficult to explain, but I've been meaning to ask; when did your lot forget we were gods? When did you forget your duty to us? Because I have to say, setting all the sacrificing nonsense to one side; the service we've been getting recently, has been bloody awful. Nothing to say? No opinion?'

Pipit tried to scream but his jaw wouldn't let him.

'Never mind, I'm sure I can work it out, given enough time; something I've got plenty of, unlike you I'm afraid my slacking servant. What's that thing you people used to say? Curiosity killed the cat? It's true, more than once I must admit. We do love investigating its true, investigating and washing, we love it, even with the occasional furball, it's well worth it. We love being clean and the process of getting clean, love it... that and playing - toying I think you call it - toying with poor defenceless animals, before we dispatch them. We love that.'

Pipit could feel his throat tightening and his windpipe closing. Inside he screamed but all the world heard was a dry, feeble, mewling.

'What's the matter poppet... cat got your tongue, that's another one of those sayings isn't it, not yet but soon, any moment now, hope you've got yourself a nice box picked out… me, I love a box.'

CAT CHAT

The tortoiseshell moggy sped across the carpark, with three dogs snapping at her tail. The safety of the high-rise block was fifty strides away, if she reached the stairs, she could lose the dogs, but she had to get there first. The dogs were only a stride behind her. The terrier to her right put on a spurt of speed and began to edge ahead; he was going to cut her off. She could feel the other two closing in, their strides were longer, they would be on her in a moment. She wasn't going to make it. A flash of red to her right, a scream and a whirr of wheels, as a messenger cyclist skidded into the fray. The tortoiseshell moggy slid sideways, dodging under the wheel, toppling the cyclist into the baying dogs. It was no more than a breath. But it gave her the space she needed, she cut left, and headed straight for the nearest wall. Go high, they couldn't reach her there, go up, go up! And up she shot, scrabbling up the last foot, to sit safe, on the hot brick ledge panting. Below her the dogs, barked and slavered, jumping up at her, teeth gnashing. But she was out of reach and safe. She turned and saw that the wall was a single structure, not connecting with anything else; a free-standing brick wall, emblazoned with the name of the high-rise estate; there was nowhere to go, she was trapped.

The three humans that had set their dogs on her were approaching, laughing at their antics. Jeers and proclamations of carnage were in the words, although she couldn't understand them, she recognised the postures and realised her peril. She spat at the snarling dogs, arched her back and ruffled-up her fur to look twice her size. But the dogs weren't buying it. They had her scent and wanted blood.

'They never learn do they,' the tabby cat with the ragged ear chuckled behind her. She was so alarmed she nearly fell from her sanctuary, sending the dogs into fresh paroxysms of murderous frenzy.

'Sorry, my fault, careful now,' the tabby entreated her with a friendly forehead nudge to her ear, 'let's not make it too easy for them shall we. What sort of dogs are those anyway? It's amazing how many tribes they have… and every single one of them an idiot. Don't get me wrong, I'm not prejudiced, I've actually met one or two I liked… but both of them were idiots. One was a huge thing… what was his name? they always have man names don't they… no its gone. But I do remember who he belonged to, which is unusual as I rarely bother knowing human names, I mean, why remember the servants. Now then let me think…'

One of the dogs ran back to its master, who launched a kick at it for its trouble and sent it back with the words; 'Sic 'um.'

'Genghis Khan that was it, the human not the dog, big slavering thing with the worst breath, the dog not Genghis, well, actually they had that in common, but he was the sweetest idiot dog I've ever met… Demon! That was it, Demon! I'm translating of course but that's close enough. A real live war dog, but if you scratched him behind the ear, he was your friend for life.'

'Mee-ooow,' the tortoiseshell replied.

'Really don't worry, they'll tire themselves out before long. The funny thing is I really got to like Demon's master too; this funny looking servant called Genghis Khan. Now obviously he was my servant, but to the other humans he was a real top cat, a force to be reckoned with; of course, Demon loved him, thought him god incarnate, which is funny, seeing as I am.'

'Miaow.'

'No really, those monkeys followed him everywhere, a whole army of them, his Mighty Mongol Hoard, that's what he called them, and they loved it. It's called being a leader. It's something men share with dogs. They love a leader; and a leader that leads them to toys and food; well they'll follow him anywhere, and kill anything they tell him to kill. Just like those idiot thugs down there.'

The idiot thugs joined their dogs in their snarling rage, charging and jumping at the wall, trying to push the cat from its perch; 'Come on kitty! Come on pussycat! Come and get yours!'

'Don't worry they can't jump. Have you seen monkeys? The little hairy ones? Now they can jump. Odd to forget something so essential, can you imagine a cat forgetting to clean itself? Now this Genghis, he had some very strange ideas about cleanliness, even for a human. He washed himself with the water from his mouth; trouble is, he didn't have much of a lick, not really his fault I suppose, but human tongues are all wrong. But when it came to cleaning those skins they wear, utterly hopeless, never washed them. Stinky Genghis I called him, maybe that's why Demon loved him, you know how dogs are about smells.'

'Meow, miaow.'

'Yes, I liked him, despite the smell. I really liked him I really did. He was good to his people and good to Demon, but then one day… we were outside this city, just another stinking human city. Genghis and his monkeys had surrounded it, like so many before, but this city refused to surrender. Now, of course this had happened before, but Genghis would normally just send in his men and raze the place to the ground. But on this occasion his men were exhausted and tetchy, weakened by sickness and many battles, and the city was very well fortified. Taking it would have cost a lot of lives; it was a problem. Genghis couldn't let the city stand against him, but he couldn't risk losing favour with his men. Not so easy being a leader you see. Poor old Genghis stayed up all night wondering what to do, with Demon at his feet and me on my rightful place of honour, a red silk pillow at the head of the bed. Anyhow, just as the sun was rising over the plain, I saw Genghis look at Demon and pat him, you know how dogs like that; makes my fur crawl; and begin to laugh; funny I thought, funny that, Genghis laughing… what's he up to then?'

'Come on kitty! Get a stick! Get a stick! Knock it down.'

'Miaow meow.'

'Humans and sticks, dogs and sticks, do you think there's a connection? So, Genghis sends this message into the city; 'Pay us the ransom of all your dogs and cats and we will let your city live.' Sounded good to me, sounded good to Demon; sounded good to the city. That very evening all the city's dog and cats and even their pet birdies were delivered to Genghis' hoard. There were a thousand cats, probably as many dogs. Fair enough I thought, that's done let's move on. But oh no; Genghis instructed his men to bind the dogs and cats and birds in tallow and wool; which they did, because he was their leader. And do you know what he did then?'

'Miaow.'

'Not even close. He set them on fire. Every one of them. The poor beasts ran back into the city looking for their masters and burnt the city to the ground. Stinky Genghis then went in and killed all the people that didn't burn to death. It was dreadful and nothing to do with me. But burning the cats, well I couldn't let that go. But the worst of it was poor old Demon, it really broke his heart. I think he lost his faith that day. He was never the same after that… one day he just wandered off and never came back.'

'On my back! Get on my back! Give it a shove. Push it off! Push it off!'

'There's two of 'um up 'ere!'

'Good! more dog food!'

'So, I waited a while, travelled a bit, decided to visit the Inca's, another odd lot. Had some fun, brought down a civilisation or two, but I knew I had to deal with Genghis one day. And so, when he was much older, I caught up with him. He was hunting, having a rare old time, him and a couple of archers. It was so easy in the end. This young archer fires a shot, it hits a tree, this alarms a swarm of bees that attack the other archer, who fires a wild shot into the sky that clips a cloud, and then plummets down to earth, landing inches from Genghis' foot. This so alarms Stinky Genghis he falls backwards into a thorny thicket, which scratches him from head to toe. A thousand cuts for a thousand cats… it didn't kill him outright, it took a couple of days, but that was fine by me, I wanted him to make the connection.'

'I'm coming kitty!'

'Meow.'

'Don't worry, I've got this…'

The mouthy yob, on the taller yob's back lunged for the moggy. Momentarily unbalanced by the sudden movement, the taller yob leant a hand on the brick wall to steady himself, just as his snapping mutt, jumped at the wall. The dog's teeth sunk into his arm, and he went flailing backwards. His piggyback buddy toppled from his back and landed on the two other dogs, who, taken by surprise in their rage, set about him with terrible vigour. Seeing this, the tall lad rushed to his jockey's aid, but being unbalanced and panicked, he fell over the dogs and dashed his head against the edge of the wall. The third yob stood silent, struck dumb, unable to move. He watched his friend's face being yanked from his skull; clutched his chest and died.

'Anyway, I better be off. It's been great to chat, not often I get the chance, you look after yourself you hear... and one last thing, love the coat.'

'Meow.'

GILES BASTET IN THE HOUSE

Giles Bastet, 9th Heavenly Cat, lord high overseer of accidental death, suspected he had acquired a flea; an irritating and persistent itch had developed behind his scraggy ear, and it was getting on his nerves, but more importantly, it was distracting him from his purpose. Already that morning, he'd watched an unbearably obnoxious Australian tourist, topple from a Peruvian mountain pass, slide headfirst down a near vertical chasm of incredible depth, drop into a jagged boulder strewn ravine, that had mangled bodies since time in memoriam; only to see the obnoxious git get up smiling. And to make matters worse, the subsequent catastrophic landslide that followed the fool into the abyss, missed its target by three yards... all due to the irritating itch behind Giles' ear. Giles didn't like to admit it, but he needed to find a human.

The cottage was as picturesque and shortbread sweet as its possible for a cottage to be. There were roses around the front gate, hyacinth around the front door, and a carpet of camomile grass between the two. But it was the delicious scent of fish and the sound of song that came from the cottage's open window that grabbed Giles' attention.

There had been a time when the human's had sung his mother's praises day and night, when fresh fish was brought to them on golden bowls and the servants' nimble fingers were at their beck and call, long time passing; it was time to relive some past glories. Giles trotted along the camomile path, cut past the rosemary and lavender bushes, and jumped up onto the cottage's windowsill. Inside was a small cluttered but not untidy kitchen; at its centre, a small hunched grey-haired woman was busy rolling pastry on a floured table. Giles announced his presence with a kingly roar; 'Meow.'

The old woman looked up, corrected the glasses that had slipped down her short nose and squinted at the window, 'hello kitty cat, smell the fish pie do you? It's not for you kitty, it's for the old folks, not for kittycats.'

'Meow,' Giles decided to play along.

'Want to come in do you? Let me get this in the oven first.'

'Meow,' Giles insisted.

'Right then let's have a look at you. Oh but you are a pretty kitty aren't you, look at you. Yes, yes, meow, meow. Oh dear, what happened to your ear?'

Why did they always have to mention his ear? Giles bristled, it was the itch behind the ear that mattered.

'Been in the wars have we? Alright, alright, come in.' Giles slipped inside. 'Oh you're not shy are you, come on in, why don't you.' Giles claimed a corner of the well-worn wooden worktop, beside the chipped Butler sink, and sat himself down.

'Let's see then shall we.' The old woman returned to her floured table, and bending almost double inspected it closely, 'Ah here we are.'

A scrap of white fish was waved beneath Giles' nose. He appreciated the offering, as humble as it was, but the practice of hand feeding was a privilege preserved for the most trusted servants. He wanted those fingers for other things, and he didn't want to smell of fish all day. So he refused the offering with a flick of his tail.

'Snooty kitty, too good for my scraps are you, well we'll see,' the scrap was placed on the worktop beside him – and seeing as the correct protocols were now being observed, Giles ate it. 'So not so snooty then?'

Giles swallowed the offering and gave his ragged ear a good scratch with his rear paw.

'Got an itch there have you kitty?'

She was a bright one, this old servant. Giles had another scratch just to confirm her observations.

'Is it a flea kitty? I don't want fleas in the house. Thank you very much.'

'Meow,' meaning – 'bother your house, I don't want them behind my ear.'

'I bet you don't want them either, well let's have a feel,' the servant's fingers reached out to touch his head; Giles turned his back on the servant and circled clear of her hands.

'What's the matter? Do they smell? Oh you're a fussy kitty. Better give them a wash first, can't have you smelling of fish, what would the other cats say?'

A very wise woman indeed, Giles rewarded her obedience with a deep purr.

The old woman washed her hands thoroughly, dried them, and then reached out to stroke Giles beneath his chin; he allowed it. 'Thing is kitty, I'll not be able to see a thing, we'll have to do it by feel. I'm afraid my eyes aren't what they used to be.' The servant's fingers brushed past Giles' whiskers, moved to his brow, and then to the space behind his ear. Bliss, oh perfect bliss. Giles had seen stars born, mountains rise and oceans flood desert plains, but a scratch behind the ear… and this is why he had to let the servant monkey men live; yes they were terrible, terrible creatures, ugly and destructive and rude; but they were so good with their fingers; next time he felt like wiping them all out it would do him good to remember this moment of…bliss.

'Ah is that it?' something was plucked from behind his ear.

The old woman held her pinched fingers beneath a jet of running water. Giles stepped closer to inspect her find; 'careful now kitty, you'll get wet and you won't like that.'

If the water was clean he wouldn't mind, but salt water beneath the fur, an image of a ship flashed through his head, when was he ever on a ship? No, he couldn't place it, but salt water in the fur, ghastly; he'd rather have a flea.

'Do you want to come through to the other room? I've got a magnifying glass in there, it helps me read. We can make sure there's no more, and the lights are better.' The old woman tottered off through the door babbling to herself as she went. Giles considered his options. He'd got what he came for; more if you counted the fish; and he didn't want to cause the old servant any harm by his presence. He wasn't a monster, the servant had served him well, he wanted to bless her, and taking himself from her presence might be the kindest thing to do. The call of 'Kit, kit, kit, kitty,' came from the other room. The room he could not see…. damned curiosity, what could be in there, what might it be? Giles just had to know. He followed the old dear into the room.

A fox glared down at him from a shelf, a badger from a glass box, and a weasel from behind a pewter tankard. Giles was surrounded. A hawk eyed him hungrily from the vantage point of its perch; and what was that? A boxing hare, wearing spectacles and a waistcoat? What was this, a coalition of foes? So, why didn't they make their move…and why was that hare wearing spectacles? Dead, they were all dead.

'Did they frighten you kitty cat? I'm sorry, I should have warned you. Don't worry they can't harm you, all long dead and stuffed as a marrow.' The old woman sat down in a rickety old chair and sighed, 'now then, let's make sure.' Lifting a large glass disk from a lopsided stool, the old woman beckoned for Giles to join her, 'come on kitty, let's make sure you haven't got any more visitors.' Giles acquiesced to her request.

Ah such bliss, an hour of unequalled pleasure, not since the days of the Old King Pharoah, not since the days of the Emperor; had he been touched like that… very heaven. Giles decided he had to find some way to reward this old servant. He would stay with her and protect her, and when her time came, he would make sure it was quick, peaceful and painless.

'Bless you, you're a happy cat. Who do you belong to then kitty?'

Belong to these servants, the very idea.

'Well, you're welcome to stay, although I can't promise fish every day.'

It's fine your garden's full of filthy birds, I can bring you one if you like.

'You're a tomboy I see and all intact. We might have to do something about that.'

I have no idea what you're saying slave, keep scratching.

'Yes you can stay and perhaps one day you'll join Marmaduke here.'

The old woman lifted the pillow from behind her back and placed it on her knee beside Giles.

Marmaduke? That's a cat? What have you done woman!

'Yes meow, meow, you look just like you're talking, I'm sure you and Marmaduke will be great friends, won't you Marmi, yes Marmi…'

That cat is dead.

'Yes meow, meow… now then I know what we must do,' the old woman fiddled with something red around dead Marmaduke's neck; removed it; and placed it around Giles' neck with a deft roll of the wrist.

By the Holy Bastet, what does she think she's doing?

'Yes, yes, meow, meow, you'll get used to it. Kitty needs a collar.'

What?

'Kitty needs a collar, good kitty, good kitty.'

Right! – 'Enough woman!'

The sinkhole that the charming little cottage at the end of Lace Lane fell into, was the top story on virtually all the TV News shows that night, well, for the first twelve hours anyhow, then it dropped to second billing after a supermodel's breast exploded on a red-carpet during London's Fashion Week. A month later the local news announcer mentioned in passing that a collapsed artesian well was thought to be the cause of the sinkhole, and that a memorial for Mrs Brody, a long-term supporter of local charities, including the local school for deaf children, was planned for the end of next month. It never happened.

GILES BASTET IN LONDON TOWN

Old London town was thick with smoke and the stink of too many people, too many horses and every other kind of defecating beast; it was horrible. A thousand plumes of smoke rose up into the night sky, only to tumble back into the cramped streets, as if the stink had caught hold of it and dragged it down to its level; truly horrible. Giles Bastet, 9th Heavenly Cat, was both fascinated – as only a cat can be – and appalled – as only a god can be – by mankind's indifference to their environment. The same creature that sniffed at flowers and planted parks filled with fabulous trees and flowerbeds; burnt down forests, poisoned rivers and filled the very air with smoke that made their offspring choke; it was baffling. In his many years of wandering Giles had seen many melodious human encampments; Babylon was ghastly, Rome was wretched and old Beijing was furball inducingly bad; but London was a whole new basket of vile. And yet, here he was right at its centre, because he had to see it, he had to know what they were up to now. And so it was, that Giles Bastet found himself wandering, one midnight dreary, through an old churchyard, alongside the River Thames, a mighty stinky river, when he heard a commotion rising from the earth beneath his feet. It was the sound of heavy breathing, the sound of toil and struggle, as something fought to raise itself from the cold earth. Giles sprang to the top of a gravestone; 'Morris Dunn Dearly Departed, Leaves His Love Broken Hearted'; and stared at the ground in fascination. The eerie sounds grew louder and louder. A beam of light burst through the ground below the church wall, as a scream of a creak broke the silent night. The figure of a man rose within the beam of light and stepped from the church's crypt, dragging two long bundles behind him. A second, shorter figure, soon followed, carrying a lantern, and dragging a single bundle behind him. Both abandoned their burdens in the darkness of the far corner of the church wall, and hurried back into the crypt; plunging the night back into darkness.

What were they up to? Giles took the opportunity to flit between the graves, and check out the bundles. He gave them a quick sniff; there could be no mistaking that aroma; spoilt, dried, man flesh. Had he discovered cannibals? Had these two miscreants popped out for a snack? Grunts and curses emanated from the earth; Giles returned to his gravestone viewpoint and watched the two panting, swearing figures, haul another load of death from the church crypt.

'We could do with a barrow,' the hunched heavy in the threadbare coat huffed.

'We could do with two sodding barrows,' his lantern carrying counterpart replied.

'How many of these sodding things do we have to shift?'

'I don't know, he said clear the space.'

'The whole thing! You're havin' a laugh. They're stuffed in there tighter than a nun's snatch.'

'Tell you what, we'll stop at fifty.'

'Fifty! No bloody chance, I'm not moving fifty of those sodding things.'

'What's the matter, squeamish?'

'No, my bloody back hurts, fifty! You never said nothing about fifty.'

'What you complaining about? a big fella like you, 'my back hurts', give it a rest; come on, we need to get this done before the tide turns.'

Both men heaved their belt buckles onto their beer bellies, and then, in perfect unison, lifted a corpse onto their shoulders, and carried it through the graves to a low wall at the far end of the churchyard. The body was then dropped over the wall, into the arms of Old Father Thames. A dead duck would have made more of a splash. A look of puzzlement passed between the men. Leaning over the wall, lantern in hand the shorter man declared, 'It's soddin' floating.'

'I told you we should have weighed it down.'

'You never did.'

'I bloody did. I told you, they're drier than sticks. Sod it. What are we going to do?'

'Nuffin', its not our soddin' problem. He paid us to clear the crypt, not to sink bodies. Let's get them in the river and get the hell out of here.'

'You're having a laugh aren't you. They'll trace the bodies back here, and I'm telling you that Verger will drop us in it, sure as day is day.'

A moment of consideration was needed. Giles watched as the men leant against a headstone, filled their pipes and attempted to think.

'You got a hammer?'

'What you thinking?'

'We break up a couple of headstones, tie them to the bodies, chuck 'um over; job done.'

'Don't be daft we'd clear the sodding graveyard.'

'Not if we tie them together, bundle them up like, ten at a time with a stone at the centre.'

'Think about the bloody noise. It's bound to get some Peelers attention.'

'Good point... what we need is an old barge... if we had an old barge we could fill it with stiffs, pull it out into the river and burn the lot.'

Giles couldn't help thinking this sounded like a very good idea. The proper way to honour the dead. Perhaps he'd got these chaps all wrong. He decided to give the men a hand. A blue flash skipped across the river.

'What was that? Did you see that?'

'I was hoping you hadn't.'

A faint meow sounded from the river below. The lantern carrier peered over the wall, 'bugger me, will you look, it's a moggy with an old barge.'

'You're havin' me on!'

'I ain't, look it's a little fella with a torn up ear.'

'Not the cat, the bleedin' barge. Ahoy. Ahoy anyone onboard?'

Meow – was the only reply.

'Oh my giddy aunt… what we waiting for?'

Giles sat on the helm of the barge as his tail curled around his body approvingly. Honouring the dead might have been an odd foible, left over perhaps from his days in Egypt, but he did believe the way a society respected its dead somehow mattered, but as he pondered this, an older, thinner memory formed in front of him… the whiff of incense, billows of smoke and the sound of a slow flowing river, intercut with incantations and the songs of mourning.

And there he was, back in Varanasi, sitting on an ash sprinkled ghat, on the banks of the mighty Ganges; how on earth had he forgotten the Mother Ganges? The river of life, receiver of death, surrounded by busy people, busy with death. The smell of burning wood and ghee, and something less appetising within the smoke. There had been an old priest, a Bramha, standing on the ghats leading down to the river, and there was a young woman, full of tears, dressed in rags and covered in the dirt of poverty and mourning; 'Bless me Brahma, bless me Brahma, my only son has died, a babe in my arms.'

'Bless you daughter. May you find comfort from your sorrows, and his spirit rise to a higher plain.'

'Please, I do not have the money to honour him as I should, please would you…'

'My dear girl, go to the temple, fear not, they will make all arrangements for you.'

'Shouldn't a father honour his own son? You remember me Brahma; the day you visited my village. You said you could heal my monthly pains. And you did for nine months.'

Within a blink, the old man's eyes turned from holy kindness to earthly rage; 'Unclean woman!' he screamed, as he raised his stick above his head, and brought it down hard across the girl's neck. Giles had just been there to watch the river and curse the birds, he didn't want to get involved, but as Mother Bastet (Blessed be her name) often said, 'to do nothing is to agree with the aggressor,' and Mother was always right.

The woman slumped forward and rolled down the step. The old man swung again and missed. Thrown off balance, the old man's foot missed the edge of the step; and down he went – head to stone – rolling over – head to stone – rolling over - head to stone – rolling over - headfirst into the flaming pyre – and there he was, gone.

Giles skipped down the steps and stood looking down on the young woman. She'd never lose another son or see another dawn. The random nature of the servants' lives baffled him. They had the power to create life and to end that creation, and they treated both gifts so casually.

A shrill whistle called through time. 'Stand still, police officer!' The cry brought Giles back to the bundle laden barge. Another shrill whistle blast brought three more uniformed men to the scene; 'I said stand still, police officer.'

'What you got Smithy?'

'These two scoundrels trying to make off with a barge that doesn't belong to them.'

'We didn't nick it, it just drifted here, honest it did!'

'A likely story… you can tell it down at the station, come on out of there.'

'Not likely…' the big chap shouted; and threw himself out of the barge and into the water.

Giles couldn't help thinking the big man should have taken off that heavy overcoat first; he came up once, pounding the water and struggling for air, and never came up again.

Panicked, his smaller compatriot ran to the other side of the barge, fell across the loaded corpses, and dropped his lantern. The barge exploded into a tower of searing flame.

Giles sauntered through the flames, wondering how such a thing could happen. Had he wanted the whole lot to go up in purifying flames? No, his intentions had been completely benign, he was shocked his intervention had ended in such a violent manner. Not perhaps, as shocked as the Peelers who watched a flame covered pussycat sedately walk along the River Thames and disappear in a blue flash under Tower Bridge, but who's to say who's experience is the most vivid, and who's burden is most trying? All I'm prepared to say is this, we can't expect an ancient cat deity to recognise a coal barge with years of coal dust in its seams. And the god of accidental death, no matter how good his intentions, can't be other than he is.

MRS DILLY-DALLY-DOO

Mrs Dilly-Dally-Doo decided to catch breakfast herself. For Lucy had her work cut out for her. The doors would be taken off their hinges; for Durtnall's men were expected. And then, thought Kitty Dilly-Dally-Doo, what a morning – fresh as if served to kittens on a red silk pillow.

What a treat! What a pounce! For it had always seemed to her when, with a little squeak of the cat-flap, which she could now hear, she had burst through the French windows and plunged out into Belton, out into the open air. How fresh, how fizzy, crisper than this of course, was that night air; like the swish of a claw; chill and sharp and yet (for a kitten of eight weeks as she was then) savage, feeling as she did, standing there on the doorstep, that something awful was about to happen; looking at the flowers, at the trees with the buzzing of insects all about them and the rude rooks rising, falling, shouting out obscenities; standing and looking until that Peter Pug had yapped at her and quite made her lose her wits. Peter Pug who bit the manservant on the leg and had to be taken to the vet, and never came back. How strange that she should think of him now, when a million other things had utterly vanished – to think of Pug, how strange it was! – a yapping dog with a face like a cabbage.

The birds were singing in Greek again, saying the same thing they always did, the filthy foulmouthed little brutes, but she wasn't going to let them spoil her day. Damn the birds, what did she care? She'd have her fun tonight. Eating her tea before the little monsters in the cage. One day they will be mine. The Mistress is fattening them up for me I'm sure of that. Damn the birds, bet they'd like to know what I had for tea, bet they don't know what I'll be having for tea again tonight, chicken with extra gravy too, no doubt. Filthy mouthed, dirty little brutes. Damn the birds, their day will come.

Mrs Dilly-Dally-Doo looks across to the park and sees a female woman, head in her hands crying. What a thing to do on a day like this? The poor dear must be hungry, or lost. To be lost in London what a thing to happen, never stray too far, follow the paths, sniff the signs and you'll always find your way home. Or just find another. But not her, no, well fed and content, happy with her servants, even if today they had other things to do, can't be helped. Makes a nice change. Exhilarating sense of independence. The kitten within, such a pounce of a day. She stiffens a little on the kerb, as she waits for Durtnall's van to pass.

A charming cat, Giles Bastet thought of her (knowing her as one does all those made in your image); a touch of the Persian about her, jade of eyes, blue-green, light, vivacious, though she was over eight human years, grown plump on pampering. There she perched, never seeing him, waiting to cross, fluffy and bright. On her way to the park to catch her own breakfast because her maidservant had enough to do that morning. A good cat, a kind cat, distracted, not really looking where she's going, lost in her own thoughts. And here comes Durtnall's van, clipping the curve, riding up onto the pavement.

How many years in Westminster? How many times had she crossed this road, on the way to the park? To cross the road before Big Ben…

And gone. Another kitty cat, roadkill. Nine lives, if only it were true. He should know, he was the source of that myth, the 9th heavenly son, the last undying son. Here comes Lucy, the crying maidservant, weeping for her mistress. As it should be. Some may say you shouldn't have been so busy Lucy, but nobody but Mrs Dilly-Dally-Doo made those choices. The van driver, inconsolable, weeping, hand on chest, pain in arm, having to sit down, to catch his breath. Will he? Perhaps not, someone has to pay. Call the gardener. Pick her up, carry her inside. Turn away Durtnall's men, cancel the party, stop all the clocks. Dig a hole in the garden beneath her favourite tree. Tell Margret the cook to save the chicken. Mrs Dilly-Dally-Doo won't be needing tea.

GILES BASTET TAKES TO THE ROAD

Giles Bastet, 9th Heavenly Cat, lord high overseer of accidental death, son of Holy Bastet, Goddess of Protection, sat on the roof of the motorway service station, soaking in the sunshine. It was a good day to be a god, the roof tiles were heating up nicely. The air teemed with buzzing life and below him in the car park his subjects came and went in their moving metal boxes, oblivious to his presence, which is just how he liked it. The world was busy, but Giles was having none of it, he was far too busy washing the holy hairy body to be bothered with the world of men; lick, lick, nibble lick – streeeetch and settle down.

Below him a family exited their little red sarcophagus; mother, father and a blonde-haired little girl carrying what looked to be a stuffed pink toy shark. The girl held her mother's hand as she skipped along, happy in the world that embraced her. As Giles yawned, the little girl's sandal caught the edge of a paving stone and the child fell forward. Calamity was narrowly avoided as the mother yanked the child aloft, catching her up in her arms. The child balled for a second; shocked rather than hurt; but as she settled into her mother's embrace, the child pointed to where Giles sat on the roof, and with a pouting scowl fixed the blame for her tumble squarely on Giles' shoulders; pronouncing loudly, 'No cat no.'

Giles was taken aback; he was innocent of any involvement, to be falsely accused is an injustice that's hard to bear, but there was something else in the girl's childish accusation that awoke an old memory that cramped his tabby tail. The face of a little girl he'd met in the palace of the Old Pharoah superimposed itself on the scene; what was her name? A sweet little thing with coal black hair, and cheeks that were permanently streaked with mud. She'd brought him fish heads for lunch and sang him songs as he ate; what was her name? But that was it, she didn't have one, he never knew it, but he'd given her a name, what was it now, what did he call her... Panya? Yes, that was it Panya, deneg Panya, little Mouse. He hadn't thought about her for ... since before the pyramids were capped; poor deneg Panya. Giles Bastet was not usually given to nostalgia. Being a heavenly being meant he had far too much past to call upon, and after a while the repetitious nature of the Zen now, rendered visiting the past redundant, but the memory of little Panya caught like a furball at the back of his throat. For weeks the dirty faced child in the dirty cotton apron, had brought him fish heads and sang him songs, while he ate from her lap, and then one day, there were no more fish heads, no more songs, no more tickles under the chin; there she was gone, and Giles, knew not where. If there's one thing a cat, be he a god or not, cannot abide it's a mystery; as his great Holy Mother used to say, 'if Isis hadn't meant us to be curious, she wouldn't have given us whiskers.' And yes, Giles was well aware that curiosity killed the cat, but he was immortal, and he needed to know, curiosity was in his whiskers.

Where to start? Giles was confident the fish heads came from the Pharaoh's private kitchen, they had to be as they were so beautifully coloured. Therefore, it followed that Panya was a scullery slave, a pan scrubber or a firepit skivvy; the thought dried Giles' throat. What if she'd fallen into the firepit? Had he spent too long in her presence and inadvertently doomed her to a fiery death? He wasn't a monster, he was a god and making offerings to gods should ensure some form of protection; at least for a while, if not what was the point? If accidents happened despite their faithfulness, people would lose their faith in the gods, and what state would the world be in then?

Giles made his way through the palaces' smoky narrow corridors; oil lamps are just accidents waiting to happen; past guards, eunuchs, and slaves, through the dusty back corridors that only cats and priests frequented – and there, as usual, in the darkest corner was Azzel Az Azzel, on his knees, vigorously blessing some ageing priest with his attentions. Giles was grateful, honouring his own name didn't require such devoted attention; just imagining the manner of the deaths that would occur, made him gag. Giles reached the entrance to the palace kitchen; and found his way blocked by a forest of serving girls' legs. Beyond the slim brown legs, a raised voice was accusing someone's mother of sleeping with a donkey and birthing an idiot; such accusations were commonplace around the palace but as their priests worshipped half men, half bird creatures he really couldn't see the problem. Amused and shocked by the ferocity of the tirade they were hearing, the gathered serving girls, simpered and giggled as only serving girls can. Giles pressed forward, snaking his way through their calves, until he found himself standing before a cowering youth, stripped naked and shaking from nose to toe, as the head cook, a loud man with a pendulous belly, threatened him with a bloodied meat cleaver.

Keeping to the walls Giles searched the kitchen from one end to the other, he checked the firepits, the spits, the bread ovens and the meat cupboards. He even checked under the tables; there was lots of dirt and dead flies but no Panya. The loud man with the pendulous belly suddenly bellowed like a maddened water buffalo; 'there's a cat in the Pharaoh's kitchen!' Kicking the quaking youth to the floor, the head cook came after Giles with a raised boning knife. Giles just wasn't in the mood; his tail twitched towards the firepit, and a bubbling shallow pan spat a thread of hot oil across the room; it landed in the fat man's eye with a sizzle. Grabbing at his head with a reactionary jerk; the fat man stabbed himself in the eye with the boning knife. Screaming in pain he careered into a wall – driving the blade through his head. Falling backwards into the firepit, his colossal bulk sent pans, coals and hot oil spinning across the kitchen floor. The oil ignited. Pandemonium ensued, some cooks ran to their fallen comrade, some ran from the sizzling fat, whilst others, the soles of their feet already seared, hopped onto counters, or ran for sand to staunch the flow of the burning oil. Giles considered his options; it was too good an opportunity to miss. A twitching whisker breathed life into the flames. Whips of fire lashed the walls; the kitchen instantly transformed into a consuming oven. Giles latched onto the back of a burning cook, as he stumbled back down the corridor, knocking the oil lamps to the floor as he went – Giles always knew they were trouble – turning this way and that, until he fell through a door into the good clean sand, beneath a bright blue sky.

A swarm of slaves formed around the Pharaoh's Kitchen Pond; frantically dipping buckets into the water and running back to dampen the blaze. Giles was indifferent and unamused, preferring to stare into the water and the thrashing fish within it. As he did so, a strange itch rippled down his back; the fish were wrong; the fish in the Pharaoh's Kitchen Pond were grey colourless Nile fish. Whilst the fish he had taken from little Panya's hand were bright orange or white as snow. Giles' whiskers drooped, and his haunches felt stiff and tired. He knew what had happened. Little Panya had not been feeding him from the kitchen pond but from the Pharaoh's own ornamental pond. She probably wasn't a servant at all, just some ragged little street urchin that had sneaked into the palace garden, perhaps she'd even hidden out there for a few weeks before being discovered; probably whilst standing in the Pharaoh's ornamental pond; her dirty apron full of the Pharoah's prized fish. Poor little Panya, what terrible fate had they bestowed upon you? Thrown into a pit of snakes? Dragged out to the desert to die of thirst? Or did they hand you to the Pharaoh's guards to do as they willed ... or possibly, just possibly was that all yet to come?

Giles turned his back on the pond and watched the thinning ribbon of smoke rising from the palace kitchen. The fire was already dying, the stone walls of the palace both intensified and contained the flames – and perhaps it was for the best, it wasn't for him to exact revenge. He was not the cat god of retribution, merely the 9th heavenly cat, god of accidental death, he must not overstep his royal duties. What did one little dead street urchin matter? Time to move on.

As Giles mused upon the limitations of godhood, a huge grey muzzle gently nudged him aside and began noisily lapping up the pond water. It was a donkey, a rather forlorn and worn donkey, with bandy legs that looked as if they would buckle at any moment.

'You'll get a thrashing for that,' Giles observed.

The donkey looked askew at the talking tabby beside him, 'I didn't know cats could talk.'

It was Giles' turn to be amazed, 'I was certain donkeys couldn't.'

'They can't,' the donkey observed, 'I however am Dead Balaam's donkey, and I do... but not much. I never really saw the point. Never had much to say.'

'That's your name? Dead Balaam's donkey?'

'I was Balaam's donkey, but he died. So, I am Dead Balaam's donkey.'

Giles' tail began to tingle in a most pleasurable way, 'it occurs to me that a talking donkey could do himself a lot of good in a land that worships animal gods.'

Dead Balaam's donkey returned to his drinking.

'There really isn't a thought going on in that head of yours is there.'

'I'm thirsty… is that a thought?'

'No not really; how did you learn to talk?'

'I didn't, it just happened. As I recall, Balaam had to be told something, I was told to tell him, so I told him.'

Giles scratched his ragged ear, it was a world of strange wonders, who was he to question such happenings. He gave the donkey a good looking over, 'you're falling apart Dead Balaam's Donkey, I think the next load you carry will kill you.'

'It's true, I am practically dead. My knees hurt, my back aches and my hooves have split; and I'm very nearly dead. It's alright for you cats, you've got nine lives but us donkeys only have one, and it's a hard life, very hard and too short.'

'Well actually I'm a god so… its even better than that. But I get your point, what if I could guarantee your last few days were spent in total comfort.'

'Comfort?'

'All the water you can drink and all the straw you can eat.'

'I would like that very much cat god.'

It took Giles the rest of the day and all that night to teach Balaam's donkey what he should say, and they were the longest, most frustrating hours of his entire immortality, donkeys are not good students – but eventually Dead Balaam's Donkey was ready.

Giles and Dead Balaam's Donkey were waiting on the wooden jetty as the line of white robed priests approached to make their sunrise offerings to the Nile. Giles could see their consternation at seeing a bloody great donkey occupying their allotted spot. A number ran ahead of the procession and attempted to shoo away the beast of burden, but as they came closer they saw Giles sitting on the animals back, and this gave them pause for thought – just enough for Giles' claw to trigger the donkey's act.

'Woe to you priests of Rai, woe to all Egypt, for the beloved servant of the Holy Mother Bastet has been taken.'

The priests fell to the floor in supplication. Giles prodded the donkey once more, and he had to admit Dead Balaam's Donkey's performance was word perfect and really rather affecting, 'Woe for the little fish girl! Who took the little fish girl from the Pharaoh's garden?'

The priests huddled together, speaking in hushed urgent voices. And then one stepped forward and knelt before the donkey, 'Blessed one, if you mean the little girl that was found stealing fish from the Pharaoh's Pond. She is dead. The Pharaoh himself observed her crime and ordered her beheading. Her body was taken out to the desert. I do not believe her suffering was great.'

Giles' fur stiffened, and he jabbed the donkey a little more harshly than he intended to; 'That hurt... go now, go now, I care not for your offerings today, seek me not!' the donkey was really giving it some gumption, 'Heed me, heed me, as penance for this act of cruelty this Dead Balaam's Donkey, that's me Dead Balaam's Donkey, must be honoured as a Pharaoh to the end of his days... that means water and straw... I have spoken... that was me speaking.'

'Nicely done,' Giles mewed into the donkey's ear as he dropped from its shoulder, and the priests ran forward to embrace their new charge.

Balaam's Donkey was immediately led away by the genuflecting priests, into the presence of the King of Kings, the living Godhead, Ra made flesh, Pharaoh. And Giles Bastet followed on, high in the palace rafters.

From his vantage point high above the holy throne, he watched the Pharaoh and his sister wife receive the holy donkey with a mix of ceremonial pomp and great alarm. The Pharaoh was clearly shocked that his authority should be questioned by a mere donkey, and therefore required proof of divinity, and so demanded that the beast speak directly to him. The priests, concerned that the Pharoah's behaviour would further insult the deity began bestowing gifts upon its holy body; garlands of flowers, jewels, a golden embroidered cloak, chains of gold, alabaster jars full of oils, balms and sweet honey; all were piled onto the beast, but it kept its silence. The Pharaoh's displeasure rose from chagrin to rage; 'Talk donkey talk! Your Pharoah commands you! Talk damn you talk!'

But Balaam's donkey said not a word; perhaps it took a god's will to induce the beast to talk or perhaps he was too tired and too weary to try. Giles observed a misshapen clump of sand and dust sitting beside him on the rafter's edge. It annoyed him; it didn't need to be there, he fixed his gaze upon it and scowled. And what was this thing? a coagulation of detritus and oil smoke residue, how fitting, that man's filth and man's industry should besmirch his greatest achievement, the Pharaoh's palace. Giles batted the dirt from its perch. It fell swift and silent, straight onto the back of Balaam's donkey. The donkey's knees quivered, as its withers withered, and betrayed its stubborn constitution. The beast tottered forward, lowered its head in supreme surrender and fell forward, collapsing to the floor with a clatter and a dull thud – which was followed by a rumbling, elongated and earthy fart. Driven back in alarm by the necrotic stink an elderly priest caught the hem of his robe with his heel, and went face first into the steps that led to the holy thrown, gashing his head open and splashing the holy ankles of the Pharoah's sister wife with his blood and brain matter. Understandably shocked, the good queen sister wife screamed in horror, jumped out of her throne and ran from the scene; it should be understood that the good queen sister wife was only twelve years old, and certainly shouldn't be blamed for her behaviour. Unfortunately, brain matter being what it is – incredibly slimy stuff – the poor child slid across the marble stairs straight into a cohort of palace guards that were running to the Pharaoh's assistance. She was skewered by three pikes through her young and undeveloped chest. The Pharaoh, seeing his child bride, sister wife, shuddering her last breath out on the end of a pike, reached for his ceremonial dagger and charged the royal guard – which was his god given right – he had however ignored the effect the toxic fumes from the dead donkey were having on his priests. Many fled, several fainted but three vomited, including Azzel Az Azzel, who due to his spirited pleasuring of many members of the higher priesthood, had a superior gag reflex, which enabled him to projectile vomit across the Pharaoh's projected path. This combination of blood, bile and brain matter turned the marble stairs from a sliding hazard into a zone of inevitable treachery. The Pharaoh fell to his knees, rolled down the steps and landed nose to muzzle with the dead donkey; just as poor Azzel Az Azzel – now completely desolate threw himself onto the dead donkey in utter dismay – forcing a jet of phlegm, bile, pond water and partially digested straw through the donkey's mouth and into the Pharaoh's face – causing the Old Pharaoh to choke and die of inhaled donkey snot; which I'm sure you'll agree is an inglorious death for such a mighty ruler. From that point on, not even 'Giles Bastet 9th heavenly cat, lord high overseer of accidental death,' could keep track of the ensuing chaos; guards fell on their swords, priests fell on guards (alive and otherwise), and slaves – seeing their chance - fell on priests, the holy family, and its entire entourage. Blood was spilt, oil was spilt, and the spark of rebellion, fuelled the flames of purification that rose through the palace and its temples as if they were so much dry kindling – which of course, Giles mused as he sauntered across the palace garden; is all any repressive regime ever is. However, he did wonder, if perhaps, he'd overreacted. But as the smoke billowed about him and the cries of the dying and the maimed filled his ears, he told himself it was probably for the best, empires and dynasties are all very well while they last, but it's the accidents that create the contours of fate; accidents are the checks and balances that no mortal man can payoff.

Four thousand or so years later, Giles Bastet watched the little girl with the stuffed pink shark, being carried back to her family's little red sarcophagus; singing sweetly as she went, and then, just as her mother bent down to place her in the car, the child's eyes found him on the roof. She raised a hand and blew him a kiss. Giles didn't flinch, he was a cat, he didn't care for such things. But in his cat's eye mind; he did check the thread of the third wheel-nut, – they'd be fine, at least till they end of that day's journey.

CAT VS BIRD

It was a beautiful day, and Giles Bastet, 9th Heavenly Cat, was enjoying his prowl through an uncut meadow, lush with flowers. It was such a beautiful way to spend a day, sidestepping a dandelion, brushing against a buttercup; focused on the thrill of the hunt, enjoying just being a cat. Giles' ears were suddenly assailed by the sound of raised voices. Looking to his left he saw a group of men on the edge of the meadow, dressed in green wax jackets jumping up and down, waving their arms in the air. What on earth were they doing? A flock of birds rose from the grass and began circling above his head, shrieking their obscenities. Moments later they were dive bombing him, insulting his mother and his lineage, in their usual disrespectful manner. The men in the green jackets began cheering, one or two even threw stones at him. Although none found their mark, Giles decided to retreat and headed for a hedge at the far side of the meadow. He heard the men cheer and curse that; 'Bastard cat.'

Passing through the hedge, Giles found himself in a gravel clearing containing a number of parked cars. Another group of humans were standing around talking. When they spotted Giles, they began kicking gravel at him, and chasing after him with clapping hands. Giles just wasn't in the mood for a confrontation, and so followed the gravel track away from the cars, until he found himself standing by a road, under a large wooden sign – which Giles, being a cat, couldn't read – it said, 'Seas End Bird Sanctuary.'

Later that same day Giles wandered into a small garden to find a mass of birds attacking a food offering, hanging from a wooden cross set into the earth. Spotting him the birds immediately began their tirade of insults. No longer able to bear the barrage of insults he'd had to endure that morning, Giles jumped at the twittering monsters. The cowards took to the sky, screaming their alarms. A moment later a jet of water hit Giles in the face, and an old man began shouting at him from his window; 'Leave my birds alone! You bastard cat!'

His birds? Was the old man mad? This was not the first time Giles had encountered the inconsistency of human affections towards birds, and it was a cause of great consternation to him. Humans ate birds; just as he did. They chased them from their crops; as he did. And yet they fed the little monsters and assaulted his holy body to protect the bastard things. What was the matter with these humans, didn't they know birds were evil?

Putting the damage they did to fruit and grain to one side. What about their foul habit of defecating all over the place? Their constant ear-splitting chattering. The awful blasphemy of their language; 'This is mine! I'm king! This is mine! I'll kill anybody that says otherwise!' And what about the things they said about humans – didn't humans know what they were saying about them? And most birds were homicidal maniacs, they'd kill anything smaller than them. He'd once been on an ostrich expedition with a young pharaoh, when one of the hideous birds disembowelled a man before the Pharaoh's very eyes; did the pharaoh kill it? No, he did not. He took it back to the palace and dressed it in gold. There was nothing that young fool liked more than feeding the damn things from his own hand; insanity. And what about eagles, hawks, and owls, they'd eat anything they happened upon; mice, rats, goats and even kittens – the murdering bastards. He'd seen vultures, crows, and eagles which humans venerated, neck deep in rotting corpses. And he'd heard it said that they ate their own young, and that wasn't the worst of it, they'd even eat their own kind. Birds were disgusting indecent creatures! Waterfowl shat in the water they swam and ate from, and the sexual proclivities of ducks were downright indecent – and yet, humans let their children feed them! Yes, Giles knew some birds were vegetarians, but these were the very one's humans chased from their fields – into their gardens where they fed them from their own kitchens, it was utter madness, idiocy.

The old man levelled his water pistol at Giles and fired. Another jet of water hit Giles squarely in the chest. The birds circling above him, mocked and insulted him with their cackling calls. It was too much too bear. Giles retreated into the garden's hedge and proceeded to seethe.

Mr Baker readied himself for bed by carefully edging his crooked feet into his backless slippers. He then proceeded to unplug the television, lock the backdoor, check the chain on the front door, turn off the mains to the electric cooker and check all the ground floor windows – twice. He then climbed the stairs, turned off the landing light and retired to his room.

As he turned on the light, he was aware of a misplaced sound, and an uncommon chill in the room. The window was open, and sitting on the windowsill was a small tabby cat, the same cat he'd chased from his garden that very morning. Mr Baker opened his mouth to berate the animal, but his voice dried to a gasp – for standing on his bed was an enormous bird with a bright blue neck, and a huge bony crop on its head.

Mr Baker knew his birds. Mr Baker knew he was in trouble. The bird fixed its dead eyes on him and leapt from the bed like a ninja warrior, its inch long talons to the fore. Mr Baker fled the room, reached the top of the stairs, turned to see his attacker, twisted his foot in his backless slippers and clattered headfirst down the stairs. He was dead before he hit the floor.

Giles watched the cassowary worry the body for a minute or two and then addressed it from the top of the stairs; 'you done reptile?' The bird replied with a low hissing rumble. Giles wasn't fluent in the local tongue, but he got the gist, and birds always said the same thing; 'I'm king, I'm king, keep away, I'll kill you!'

'Come on then your highness, let's see what you're made of...'

The cassowary lifted its besmirched claw, lowered its head and exploded into a ball of fluff and meat tainted feathers.

Giles watched the feathers drift through the air and settle over the corpse.

Yes, after all, it had been a beautiful day.

CAT STORY

The tavern was hot and stuffy, thick with tobacco smoke, sweat and the heavy scent of stale spilt ale. But the fire in the grate kept being fed, it was a cold night beyond the walls of the Slaughtered Lamb, and darkness and cold had to kept at bay, but try as they might the weary travellers who gathered around the hearth could not keep one thing at bay, fear.

'It was Old Shug I'm telling you what I saw.'

'You saw nothing but a black shape on the highway.'

'It was a dog I'm telling you.'

'Then a dog it was, that don't make it Old Shug, there's plenty of stray dogs about days thanks to the plague.'

'It was an enormous dog, unnaturally large.'

'Like a horse you mean.'

'It weren't no horse!'

Voices rose as beer tankards thundered against tabletops, beer was spilt and blood would surely follow, but then a broad shouldered with a thick scar that ran from his right eyebrow to his chin, took off his heavy boot and began to bash its heel repeatedly against the chimney breast. The crowd quietened, 'you got something on your mind stranger?'

'It's a dark and foreboding night, let us not sour the hour of kinship but lighten it with a tale and a song.'

A chorus of approval rippled across the tavern.

'And besides, it's not Old Black Shug you should be concerned with, but the Raggedy Eared Cat. Do you not know of the Raggedy Eared Cat?' A murmur and a rush for seats and laps to sit on followed. 'In that case, if you're so inclined, I'll tell you of the Raggedly Eared Cat of Death. Now you see, long ago, far away in the land of the Pharaohs, where God's servant Moses was born. Man practised idolatrous ways. He worshipped false gods, demons with the heads of birds and animals and the bodies of men. And one of these gods was the cat headed goddess Bastet. Now being a shapeshifting demon, she sometimes appeared as a cat, so people there honoured this false god by worshipping cats. They built temples for them and fed 'um and when they died, they honoured their body just as if they were the Pharaoh himself.'

'It ain't so!'

'It bloody is, you go up to the manor house in Gunby and ask to look at the Squires antiquities, he'll show you a dead cat all wrapped in bandages and covered in gold, just like a Pharoah.'

'And then he'll shoot your arse for asking.'

'Well, that's as maybe. But I swear its true. Now Queen Bastet, had herself a litter of kittens, nine in all. She gave each one a secret name and a deadly task and sent them out into the world to reap discord and destruction on mankind.'

'Why?'

''Why what?'

'Why reap discord and destruction?'

'They're demons, what other reason do they need? Now the last of the nine, the smallest of the litter…'

'Runt.'

'And that he was, never a truer word spoken. A right royal runt at that, but Queen Bastet favoured him above all the others and gave him a special gift, he was to be the harbinger of accidental death.'

'That's not much of a blessing.'

'Do you think not? Not for us that's for sure. For it means if you should see this cat, or God forbid, stop to pet and talk to him, you'll be dead before the day is out. And your death… will be most horrid, violent and cruel. The farmer that falls upon his own ploughshare, the drayman who falls under his own team, their blood will feed the field and flow in the street, for stopping to see the Raggedy Eared cat.'

'How did it get the raggedy ear?'

'It was an angel. God sent the Archangel Michael to gather up the children of Bastet in a basket. And being a mighty angel he caught eight of the demons right quick but the 9th alluded him, till one day, Michael spotted the cat sleeping in the nave of a church. He crept up on him as quiet as he could, but as he reached out to grab the scoundrel, the cat's ear twitched and he went to spring away, but Michael caught him by the ear and held him fast. Now try as he might Michael couldn't get a decent hold of the writhing creature, what with all the scratching and hissing, and twisting and turning, so Michael pinched down hard on the beasts ear, but this drove the thing wild and it broke away leaving the good Archangel Michael with nothing but the corner of he cat's left ear. And that's how you spot him, and tell him apart from the common moggy, a bit of his left ear is missing, the pinch of an angel.'

'What should we do if we see him?'

'Run! But run or sit it will make no odds if he sees you. For if he sees you, your death is as certain as the dawn.'

'Can he be bartered with?'

'What? A piece of fish if you let me live Kitty? I think not. You know cats, they like to play with their prey, he might take all of your gifts and promises, but he will not let you walk away.'

'My arse.'

Up on the roof, sitting atop the chimney stack, sat one raggedy eared tabby cat. He stretched, yawned, and curled up inside the chimney's flue. Soon the ale drinkers would feel sleepy, and the tobacco smokers would cough, the smoke would fill the ale house, and the fallen drinkers block the doors off. A spark would fly, a log would roll, and up in smoke the whole merry lot would go.

Giles loved to curl up to the sound of a good story, but remained very sensitive about his ear.

Giles Bastet
9th Heavenly Cat

Lyrics: Helen Lindley

Music: Helen Lindley

Helen Lindley

1.

For centuries I've roamed these lands, I've travelled all through time.
I wander here, I might stop there, I'll maybe stay awhile.
For as I pass through all hist 'ry, it pains me now to say,
Some humans are a nasty bunch, I wonder who'll be saved?

Chorus
Giles Bastet Cat. Son of a Goddess, Great Holy Goddess, Bastet Cat!

2.

Giles Bastet 9th Heav'nly Cat, a son of a Goddess.
Great Holy Goddess, Bastet Cat, Gran's Isis, no less.
Accidents tend to arise, especially when I'm near.
My thing is accidental death, I'm Lord High overseer.

Chorus

3.

Some accidents are awful things, the innocent are harmed.
I feel a little pity then, I'm even quite alarmed.
But satisfaction comes my way, I've skills I must confess:
My punishment of evil ones is 'accidental' death.

Chorus

4.

I lived in ancient Egypt, we cats were quite revered.
You worshipped us, you treated us like Gods, we were endeared.
How times have changed as you forget you're servants of we cats.
And though some cats are lucky ones, others treated worse than rats.

Chorus

5.

I seem a little grumpy now, it's 'cause I'm really tired.
Well, you'd be too if you were me, so maybe I'll retire.
I'll leave the humans to their fate; farewell to ev'ryone.
A whisker tweak and twitch of tail a blue flash then I'm gone!

TALKING CAT BLUES

'I'm telling you man, it was some spooky shit.'

'I understand you're frightened Mr Bloor, but please, mind the language.'

'Mind my language… are you crazy?'

'That's not a word we use here Mr Bloor.'

'Why not? It's a nut house ain't it.'

'And once again, not a phrase we encourage here Mr Bloor, it has very negative connotations.'

'Say that again?'

'We don't want to cause offense. The people here need understanding, not labels.'

'Offence? Offence! I'm the one that's been dragged into the nut house, I'm offended. I have a right to be offended, my right to free speech is being curly-tailed.'

'Well, let's see what we can do about that shall we Mr Bloor? Perhaps understanding why you were brought here, would help us in moving forward. So why don't we talk about that James? You don't mind me calling you James do you?'

'It's my name ain't it. I know why I'm here and I know why you think I'm here. It's because of that cat.'

'Among other things, yes. But to be exact, you were found in the middle of the high street, in broad daylight, naked and screaming about a talking cat.'

'With the ragged ear.'

'I beg your pardon?'

'It had a ragged looking ear, like someone had taken a bite out of it.'

'Indeed, a talking tabby cat with a ragged ear.…'

'I was running for my life. I saw the patrol car parked outside the deli and ran to it. I was seeking help and assistance, and they arrested my ass and threw me in here.'

'Because you were running from a talking cat James.'

'What was I meant to do? Pet it?'

'Indeed... tell me, do you often see talking cats?'

'No of course not.'

'Have you heard cats talking to you before?'

'No, not cats... I sometimes hear cats meowing, but not in English.'

'Of course, I suppose that's something. Tell me, did it have an accent?'

'What?'

'Did the cat have an accent? Did it perhaps sound like somebody you know?'

'No... that would be creepy. But it did sound a bit foreign... oriental maybe ... Eastern ... Russian or Jewish ... a bit Arab.'

'That's quite a range...'

'They all sound the same to me... ragheads and Jews and Japs and ... look I'm not racist, but I don't trust foreigners. My Daddy fought in the war for this country.'

'I see... and do I offend you?'

'Why? Because of your colour, no, you can't help that, that's not your fault. You're an American, same as me. I told you I'm not racist.'

'Indeed, and yet this terrifying talking cat sounded like a foreigner, do you think that could be significant?'

'I don't know... maybe that's what cats sound like, how should I know? I never heard one talk before. I'll tell you one thing, its English was perfect.'

'Purr-fect.'

'That's not funny.'

'No… sorry. Please, tell me what happened.'

'This is all confidential right? I mean I can tell you stuff, and you can't tell anybody else right… like a priest or a lawyer right?'

'As long as you're not a danger to the public James, of course.'

'I'm no danger, believe me, you've nothing to worry about from me. It all started two years ago. I've been living above Morris Map's Hardware Store for five years, no issues, no problems. Don't get me wrong, I'm no saint, never said I was, but I've been keeping my nose clean ever since that mix-up in Michigan; I know the Lord was looking after me that day, so now I keep my nose clean, my head down, and take one day at a time. Ol'Morris was good to me, gave me a helping hand when others didn't. He was like a father to me, hell sometimes I'd even watch the till for him, he trusted me to do that, and it was an honour to uphold that trust. And then Ol'Morris goes and sells the building to these Koreans, including my flat. Ol'Morris said there'd be no problem. He sold it on the understanding that I lived there, you understand, that was the agreement. It may not have been on paper but that's what Morris told me; the flat was mine as long as I wanted it. Well, straight-off it all goes South. They ripped the whole store out. Three weeks of banging and crashing, day and night, them crafty bastards split the store in two…pow… no more hardware store, now it's some foreign food store. Korean's and what-not coming and going all day and then, to cap it all, they turn the other half into a takeaway that's open till midnight. And I'm living above it, in the stink of their food all day long, it gets into everything, my clothes, my hair, I stink like a damn China man…'

'I thought you said they were Koreans?'

'Chinese, Korean, Japs, it's all the same thing. It gets so bad I can't sleep at night for the stink, and all the time they're jabbering away in their jibber-jabber. I can't stand it. And the music they play; it's enough to drive a man out of his mind. And then I figured it out;

they wanted to drive me out of my flat. They wanted me out, so they could ship another aunty over from Korea-land, yeah that's what I thought… but you know what, I was wrong, way wrong, it was darker than that, way darker.'

'How do you mean?'

'I'd been watching them see… and I knew they were up to no good. Strange goings on late at night, meetings, gatherings, real murky cult stuff… men in hoods… disturbing cries in the night. And I just knew there was something going on down there, but I couldn't prove it. And then one day I saw this boy arrive, no older than five, a fine whiteboy with blonde hair. I saw those devils take him into the shop… but I never saw him leave. And that's when I figured it out. They were holding him captive. He was a slave, like you hear about, a modern-day slave and they were keeping him in the basement, to carry out their evil deeds upon him. So that Saturday, last Saturday, real early, I snuck down into the shop, there's a door to the landing at the back of my place, I used to go in and out via the fire escape at the back of the place, but Ol'Morris kept the door there in case I needed to pop down, you know, so I could help him out…anyhow; I went down there, into the shop. There ain't nobody there, being so early, but I didn't hang around see, no I went down into the basement, which is a pretty big space you know, it's where Ol'Morris stored most of his stock, and these Korean fellas had done the same, or that's what they wanted everyone to think; coz that's where I found him, this poor young boy, tied to a bed, being held captive… needing help and assistance… which is what I was trying to do when this devil cat showed up out of nowhere. Now I don't mind cats, but I'm more of a dog man myself; I had me a big old Doberman, fantastic dog, smart as a whip, taught him no end of tricks, but anyhow, that's by-the-by, now I was just about to release this poor child from his captivity when this demon cat jumped at me and tore off my shirt, I'm telling you it was possessed. I tried to beat it away but he was too quick, next thing I know I'm walking into a big ol'can of cooking oil and it spills all over me, I couldn't get a grip on nothing I'm falling about all over the place, it was ridiculous. I had to take my trousers off, lay 'um on the floor just to have something to stand on, and then just as I'd managed to find my feet and reach that poor child in need of my assistance… that damned cat talked; straight-on-up; it talked, clear as a bell…'

'What did it say…?'

'I don't rightly recall but it was some spooky voodoo shit.'

'A cat spoke to you, and you can't recall what it said.'

'Voodoo shit man, some kind of warning, like some Satanic thing, beware and death to all white folks… real Satanic shit. That's what was going on down there; child sacrifice to that demon cat. Them Koreans got some next-level weird shit magic going on down there, it ain't Christian that's for sure, and it ain't American either, no sir, no child sacrificing for me.'

'And then what?'

'I ran away, out into the street to get help, and got my ass arrested that's what.'

'I see… and how did the boy end up dead?'

'Go ask them Korean's that, ain't nothing to do with me. I guess he died in the fire. Or maybe he was dead before I got there. He weren't moving none, you ought to be asking them Koreans that not me. I guess I was just too late.'

'And the fire?'

'I don't know… maybe that spooky cat knocked over a candle or something, like I said there was a lot of cooking oil in that basement.'

'So, you getting arrested was all a big mistake, and you're the hero.'

'That's right… but I don't think of myself as a hero, no sir, I only wish I got there in time to save that poor white child from them child sacrificing oriental Satanists.'

'So you didn't rape, torture and murder the boy. You didn't set the Korean Rose Restaurant on fire to cover your tracks, and then run out into the road to establish an insanity plea.'

'No, I ain't insane, I told you the truth. The boy was dead before I got there, and that cat was a talking demon cat, probably something those damn Koreans brought over from China with 'um.'

'I see… well thank you for talking to me James, I'm just going to step out for a moment, would you like an orderly to bring you some water?'

'I could do with a cigarette.'

'I'll see what I can do.'

'So what you think Doc?'

'One question; he mentioned Michigan. You didn't say he had history.'

'I didn't want to influence your opinion Doc. There was no conviction. They had him for attempted kidnapping of a minor, but he walked because the kid's parents had some issues with Social Services and his lawyer made it look like a case of bad parenting.'

'I see. Well in that case Detective, he's as sane as you or I, I've never seen a worse performance in my life. The man's a paedophile, a racist, and a sexual sadist. But he's also sane.'

'And that makes him a murdering bastard… funny thing about that fire though. Fire starters usually have previous.'

'He obviously intended to lay blame on the Korean family that own the shop, but something went wrong, so he decided to destroy the evidence.'

'Nearly worked to. Thankfully the waterpipe that goes through the basement burst and flooded the place, luckily for us the water never reached the body, so we've got enough DNA to put this guy away forever… personally I wish we had the death penalty. But the thing I don't get Doc is the whole devil cat story, surely it just draws attention to himself.'

'I said he wasn't mad; I didn't say he wasn't stupid. Perhaps he didn't mean to kill the boy and when he did; he needed to concoct a viable alibi...'

'And that's the best he could do? Satanist Koreans and a talking cat.'

'Again... not mad, but stupid.'

'So you don't recall what I said is that right?'

'Oh my god, how did you get in here? Help! Help! It's here, the cat is here.'

'I really wouldn't bother, they're not buying it, and neither will anybody else. I told you, your life is forfeit for your evil deeds.'

'Get away from me, get away. Help! Help!'

'Now, now; its better this way, would you really prefer to be stabbed in some shower block, or spend your days swapping fluids with the other bad boys behind bars. This way is better... and more amusing. Let me explain what's happening; two floors above us a fat man with bad breath is doing some maintenance in something called the 'sluice room'. He's just dropped his screwdriver. The trouble is, it's an old building, the floor in that room has been very poorly maintained. Too many spills, too much bacteria; the floor gets a lot of wear-and-tear, it's a ward for your discarded elderly, you see? The fat man's screwdriver has fallen behind something called a 'washer disinfector,' you humans and your names. And there goes the screwdriver down a crack between the wall and the floor... you'd think that would warn him wouldn't you? But no, not a clue, there he goes trying to shift that big, heavy piece of medical equipment, he could hurt his back... I can't let that happen; a little divine intervention is needed; so tell me James, do you remember what I said to you now?'

'Nobody abuses my name and gets away with it. But I didn't, I didn't I don't even know your name.'

'You lured that child to its death with the promise of kittens… want to see some kittens little boy… shame on you. And wait for it … there goes the floor. Don't worry the fat man has jumped clear, but the floor's coming this way and there's nothing you can do about it. Hear that? There it is, hitting the storage room above us, and that's completely overloaded with bottles of water for the water coolers and boxes of paper for that huge photocopier they keep in there, can you hear the floor straining? It's going to give… wait for it … here it comes… heads up … catch.'

PLAGUE CAT

Giles Bastet, 9th Heavenly Cat, had really fallen on his feet; it was in his nature. He'd found himself a considerate old retainer living in a small cottage on the edge of a forest, who seemed to know how to treat him with the respect he deserved. She kept the cottage clean, sweeping the floor daily with a twig brush, which made a scratch-scratch-scratching that greatly amused Giles. She was an expert at locating and removing fleas, but knew her boundaries, never pawing him more than he wanted to be pawed. It was a simple life, their abode was certainly no palace, there were no red silk pillows and no gold dishes, but he liked the simple rhythm of their simple life, it balanced his whiskers, made him feel peaceful. The daily outing to forage for mushrooms, the tending of the garden, the milking of the goat – a great goat, he loved that goat. It all gave Giles a sense of contentment he hadn't known since he'd drank from that Greek Egyptian queen's bath; what was her name? He also grew to admire the old woman's ingenuity; she grew herbs in her garden which she dried in bundles and hung from the cottage's rafters. This gave the simple dwelling a pleasant odour and created lots of dancing shadows for Giles to chase after. But the best of this, was the old dear's ability to grow a herb with truly magical properties; Giles couldn't get enough of the stuff – it made his head spin and his fur tingle; it was potent stuff, he'd never know anything like it, and the old dear always made sure he had a fresh supply. He was blissed-out most evenings. In return for her obedience, Giles kept the birds off the old girl's garden, and made sure he was never in her presence too long, just in case something untoward happened to her. And if some vile rodent dared to venture into their domain, he caught it and offered it to the old girl as a reward for her service; and bless her old crooked back, she seemed to appreciate the gesture, trading the mouse for portions of rabbit she'd trapped in the wood. Giles had to admit the whole arrangement had lifted his spirits.

'Mama Bianchi! Mama Bianchi!'

Giles watched the old woman raise herself from her seat by the fireplace and make her way to the cottage's door.

'What is it my dear?'

A young woman with red rimmed eyes was standing at the door, wringing her hands.

'Mama Bianchi, my son has a fever. It's been three days; he can't keep anything down and he's started to weaken. This morning he had a seizure, and I called the Priest; he said he had a demon. He bestowed the last rites.'

'Old fool. How old is the child?

'Five years. He's my only son. Please Mama Bianchi he's all I've got since his father…''

'Yes, yes, yes. Has he cut himself? Is there a wound?'

'Of course, he's a boy. He cut his knee playing in the river by the tannery, but that was five days ago.'

'Well, that will be it… that rivers filthy. Why didn't you come to me before?' the old woman busied herself, collecting handfuls of herbs and powders from the pots on her shelves, 'listen now, clean the wound with boiled water. Do you have wine in the house?' The young woman nodded. 'Good, use that instead. Boil a handful of this in a glass of wine and make him drink it, its bitter but it will bring his fever down. Give it morning and night. Then mix three spoons of this powder with water, boiled water and feed it to him; it will settle his stomach. Wash his body down with cool water and then, if the fever breaks, give him fresh goats milk with honey. If that doesn't work… then you've left it too late.'

'Yes Mama Bianchi,' the young woman bowed, 'what can I give you?'

'Nothing for now. If he survives bring me some eggs; and keep him away from that tannery.'

'I'll light a candle for you Mama Bianchi.'

'I'd rather you didn't. Save your money and feed yourself. You look worn out child,' the old woman closed the door and returned to her place by the fire, 'bloody fools, don't they know what goes into a tannery? I hope the mite makes it. As for that priest… damn all priests.'

Giles had rather fond memories of a few priests from the days of his youth, but he had to admit if they'd been any good at their jobs the world wouldn't be in the state it was in, and he doubted time had improved their performance. He tucked his feet under his chest, felt the warmth of the fire seeping into his fur, and dreamt of tree climbing goats with bloated udders.

Father Meloni's stomach was churning. A curse, he was sure. The bottle of wine and three veal chops, the rich sauce, and the loaf of bread he'd consumed, had nothing to do with it. He was afflicted by the devil; the question was, why did God keep letting this happen? In what way was he failing in his duties to be so burdened? A bell sounded and moments later his housekeeper came fawning into the room.

'Father, it's a deputation from the village.'

'Now? Can't these fools tell the time? What do they want Mary?'

'To see you Father.'

'Obviously…' Father Meloni bit his lip, why was he cursed with such idiots? 'Show them in Mary, show them in.'

Three men, peasants to the bone, dressed in grubby mud-spattered cloaks, dragged their mud laden boots into his dining room and bowed; 'Father,' they intoned with one voice.

'Greetings Luca, Matteo, Enzo, what do you want at this hour?'

'Forgive us Father, but we thought you should know, we've completed the task you set us.'

'Task, what task?'

Enzo, a pox faced brute who brought the stink of the stable with him wherever he went replied, 'the edict Father, the edict from the Pope, you told us of… that Christendom should be cleared of all cats, we've completed the task Father.'

'You've cleared all of Christendom of cats. I find that hard to believe Enzo.'

'No Father, not all of it. Just our bit. All the village's cats have been killed. And we wanted to know what we should do with their bodies. Is there a right way of dealing with them that won't release the demons within?'

In all truth Father Meloni didn't give a fig for the Pope's edict, but he was rather impressed by his flock's enthusiasm for the task, 'Gentlemen, I must congratulate you on your dedication to the task. Most commendable, so all the cats from the parish are dead, it's something to tell the bishop at least, I'm sure he'll be pleased gentlemen,'

The men squirmed in their muddy boots; 'not exactly the whole parish Father. Mama Bianchi who lives on the edge of the village. She still has a cat but...'

'Is she still alive? That old crone, she must be fifty years old if she's a day. Oh, we don't need to worry about that now. Leave her be, she'll be dead soon and her cat will eat the old pagan before she's cold. No, it's a good job well done men. I will write a letter to the bishop first thing in the morning, But now, if you'll forgive me, its time I retired... to my private contemplations.'

The three men looked crestfallen like children who had been scolded for whispering during mass, 'But Father, what should we do with the cats so as not to unleash the evil spirits within them?'

'Oh yes of course... let me think... burn them, send them back to hell in flames... and gentlemen, go in peace, bless you, I shall mention you in my prayers, and to Bishop Selco.' The three men beamed, bowed, and fled from the room. 'Blithering idiots,' Father Meloni, lifted a leg and farted – it was a foul curse to be sure – and cradled his stomach in both arms.

The next morning's Mass was a trial of endurance for Father Meloni, his stomach felt as if it had been squeezed in a winepress and his arse was scorched by the devil's own breath. He neglected to breakfast and decided to start his parish rounds early, so that he could retire early to his bed. The first call he made was on the young widow Gallo, her child was sick, and he'd already administered the

Last Rites, so it was better to attend the scene than be called to her hovel when he wanted to take his ease.

'Father, come in, come in,' the Widow Gallo was unexpectedly buoyant, 'what can I do for you.'

'No child, I'll not come in, bless you. I was just calling to enquire about your son, and the service we need to arrange.'

'That won't be necessary Father. His fever's broken, he's weak but eating. I think he'll be fine.'

'Thank God,' Father Meloni couldn't hide his surprise, 'a miracle indeed. The Lord be praised, I must admit I thought all hope was lost.'

'Oh, it's no miracle Father Meloni,' the girl's eyes looked him over, as if he were a weakling calf, 'just some herbs from Mama Bianchi.'

The door closed in Meloni's face, and he was left standing on the street with his wrath in his hands. Who the hell did Mama Bianchi think she was? He'd administered the Last Rites; the church and he Father Meloni, would not be mocked.

Giles was watching over the cottage from the vantage point of an oak tree branch when the men arrived on the cart. There were three of them, carrying cudgels, a pike and unsheathed swords. They beat on the door with their cudgels and demanded Mama Bianchi's present herself; 'in the name of God!' The door opened and the old woman appeared with raised broom in hand. What happened next was rapid and untidy. One of the men grabbed the old woman and tried to drag her from her cottage. She swung the broom and connected with her aggressor's head. He hit her, she spat, and he hit her again but this time with the cudgel. Mama Bianchi fell to her knees and began to call down a curse upon the man, a curse she never got to finish; the men drew their swords, and fell upon her with screams of rage. When the deed was done, they dragged the crooked bleeding body back into the cottage and seconds later, it was in flames. No more rabbit titbits, no more evenings by the fire, and no more blissing out for Giles. Had they no idea how difficult it was to find a decent servant? Had they no respect for his property? To insult his, was to insult him!

Enzo turned to his cart to see a ragged eared tabby cat sitting on the tailgate, 'I've found the witch's cat. Bring me the bag…'

'You get the bag; I'm killing the goat. You know what these witches are like. You can't be too careful,' Luca replied.

'I've already killed the goat,' Matteo laughed, 'the bags in the cart.'

Giles couldn't believe his ears; they'd killed the goat! What had the goat ever done to them! What was the matter with these animals?

'Why did you do this?'

Enzo fell to his needs, Matteo threw-up and Luca pissed himself; 'Satan!'

'No, never heard of him. My name… my name is my business.'

'Get thee behind me Satan!'

'No, and I'm not shifting for you fools. Why did you do this?'

'God told us to do it.'

'No, I did not. Why did you do this?'

'The Pope…'

'Father Meloni said…'

'She was a witch, she deserved to die! Kill the demon!'

What happened next was quick and very tidy. Matteo rushed forward sword raised, Luca rushed forward with cudgel raised, and Enzo charged the cart with pike lowered. Matteo's sword swung at Giles' head and missed because it was no longer there, connected with Luca's jugular and both were run-through by Enzo's pike.

'Holy Jesus,' Enzo whimpered.

'No, that's not it either,' Giles growled, as his unsheathed claws tore through Enzo's neck.

Father Meloni was awoken by a scratching at his window. He pushed the covers aside, lit the candle and carried it to the darkened pane. But the glass was too thick, too dark to see through – the scratching continued – Father Meloni reasoned; it must be a windblown leaf or perhaps an injured bird; and opened the window. And there was a cat, a little tabby cat, holding a rat in its mouth.

'Get away, go, get away from here.' Meloni commanded.

The cat lent forward, dropped the rat onto the floor, fixed Meloni with a soulless stare, then turned tail, and disappeared into the night. Father Meloni looked at the bloody rat at his feet and felt his stomach lurch. As he bent down to pick up the corpse by its tail something tiny and unseen jumped from the rat's cooling body onto the warmth of Father Meloni's arm and bit, passing its deadly bacillus into the Father's bloodstream.

With no cats to curb their roaming the rats flourished in the small dirty village, and in less than two weeks the plague had reduced the populace to unmarked graves and weeping mourners. When Widow Gallo and her son fled the parish, they stopped at the charred remains of the old woman's cottage and set down a basket of eggs in the ash.

'There's a cat Mama.'

'Where darling, where?'

'In the tree Mama, there Mama look, look...'

'Where baby, I don't see it.'

'It's gone now Mama, it's gone,'

THE TELLTALE CAT

Dearest Edgar,

My dearest darling love, forgive me for troubling you. I know you are busy, and have much on your mind, but I had to write, for I have a disturbing narrative that I need to relate. I hardly expect you to believe it my love. I hardly believe it myself.

I miss you terribly Edgar please hurry home, I cannot sleep without the sound of your quill scratching late into the night. And in your absence, the nights have been trials of endurance, vexing, and taxing, and all too long. I am filled with forebodings for the night to come. You left Monday morning and I retired early to bed, full of yearning, wishing the days away to quicken your return. But I awoke before the midnight hour, surrounded by silence and the unsettling sensation that I was not alone. I called out your name thinking that perhaps you had returned earlier than planned, without sending prior word, but that was wishful thinking, I lit the candle on your side of the bed and sat up to view the room. And saw nothing there. You would be amazed at your little wife's courage, for I got out of bed and searched every corner of the room, the closet, even under the bed to make sure I was alone – without a thought of what I would have done if I had not found it to be so. And although I proved to myself that I was perfectly alone, I could not escape the feeling that I was being watched. And then I heard it, a tap, tap, tapping on the windowpane. I had not understood the expression 'my heart was in my mouth,' until that moment, I could barely breathe for its pounding. But I did not flee or hide under the covers as you might think I would, no I held the candle high and pulled back the curtain. And there on the windowsill was a cat, scratching at the glass. And as soon as it saw me it began pleading to come in. How it managed to get itself in such a pickle and reach such a perilous height I can only guess, but there it was, stuck on our windowsill, tapping at the glass, begging to come in. And so of course I let it in.

As soon as I opened the window the creature stepped to my dressing table and then to the bed, where it sat washing itself as if its ownership of the bed could not be questioned. And I did not have the heart to throw it out, in truth I was glad of the company, and so returned to the bed to chat and pet the creature. But it would not let me touch it, no matter how I entreated it. It kept its distance and by way of the sternest looks made sure I kept mine. It was a most ordinary looking cat, a tiny grey thing with black stripes, utterly unremarkable except for its right ear, that had a ragged outline, as if a bite had been taken from it.

Hoping to win the cat's affection I bid it to follow me downstairs so that I could feed it, but the thing would not move, it just curled up on the bed, playing the part of a dowager expecting to be served. As it would not follow and would not let me carry it downstairs, I shut the cat in the bedroom and hurried down to the kitchen. I filled a saucer with milk and found a few scraps of mutton and hurried back up to present my gift. But when I got there, the bed was empty, the cat was gone. I searched the entire room, from top to bottom, four times or more. The cat was gone. And before you think it, I can assure you the window was still fastened. I spent most of the night searching our bed chamber and then the rest of the house for the thing, but it had gone. How, I cannot say. I can hear your voice saying; 'Could you have dreamed it?' I asked myself the same question, and I am certain I did not. I have no explanation, and this troubled me the whole day through. I spent hours of the next day searching the house anew, I even called on our neighbour, Mrs Price's young son Vincent, to help me search the house, but in the end, I had to settle on the unsatisfactory conclusion that the cat had disappeared, although I knew not how. And then came the next night, last night. Again, I retired early, earlier even as I was so fatigued by that day's intrigues and longed to sleep, but your absence was all the more evident, more profound and I could not sleep. I tossed and turned, wrapped myself around your pillow and wasted a whole candle trying to settle myself by re-reading your letters. And just as I was on the treacle edge of dreams, the sensation of being watched reformed in my mind. I searched the room and then, although I heard no sound, I checked the windowsill, and there was the cat. Sitting where it had sat, waiting for me to let it in. Again, I opened the window, and as before it hopped from dresser to bed, but on this occasion, it did not settle down to wash but sat at the end of the bed watching me, most intently. At first, I thought it wanted my attention, and so I tried to pet it but again it shunned me and ignored any entreaties for affection. Again, I thought about feeding it, but was loathed to leave it alone in the room again, lest it might repeat its retreat and leave me with another day of pondering, but eventually I had to forsake any attempt to cajole it to the kitchen, and so, I went like a serving maid to the larder to fetch milk and mutton. But on this occasion, when I returned the cat was still there. Sitting bolt upright on the bed, like a general taking the salute of his troops. I set the food before the cat and I might as well have set a dictionary before it, it didn't even deign to sniff my offering. A haughty kitty indeed. As it would not eat, and would not be petted, I made myself comfortable and determined to talk myself to sleep in its company. And all I can say is, there has never been a more courteous cat. Neither political orator, nor Methodist preacher have enjoyed a more attentive audience. I talked till my head was dizzy and thick with sleep. And then I slept; and this is the worst of it, for I dreamt of the tabby cat. He had a voice and a story to tell. He apologised for his behaviour and informed me that his actions were not personal, and that any distress he'd caused me was not malicious but merely his nature. He asked me to forgive him for his intrusion and insisted that the purpose of his visits would greatly benefit the minds of men, although he admitted it would do me harm if he spent too long in my presence. But he promised there would be no pain, although he swore that you my beloved would carry the burden of his visitation to your grave. It was the strangest and most lucid dream I have ever known. Once his apologies were made, the cat entertained me with tales of the Orient, Egypt and faraway lands where goats climb trees. He spoke most eloquently of a place called Bekonscot that sits beside the sea? A place of little houses that time has frozen in a moment; have you ever heard of anything so bizarre? I know it's all too fanciful and preposterous to be true, but I swear I recall the conversation with perfect clarity. But come the morning light, the cat was gone – I have turned the house upside down to find how or where he went, but the cat is gone, and I know not whether where he went?

And now I am tired, worn most thin. My shoulder hurts, my ankle aches, and my head rattles as if there were a stone within. That's something I neglected to say - on the second night, last night, on my visit to the larder, I tripped on the flagstone. A bang on the head, as my Mother often said, 'to make me a little smarter.' Nothing of any significance, a slip, a trip and a bump to the brow, nothing more, though it does seem to throb after so much writing. Perhaps trying to write in the dim early morning light was not the wisest thing to do. I will resign myself to missing you, wish you adieu, and entreat you to return as soon as you can. If the cat returns tonight this will be my third sleepless night, my third night away from you - hurry home my love, I want you to meet this mischievous tabby cat. I shall name him, and you can write a story about him. How odd, now that I think of it, I'm sure the cat informed me of his name - Giles, is that not a perfectly peculiar name for a cat? I am tired and sorely missing you. The moon is full tonight. We may not be together to share it but if you look up at midnight and I do the same, we will be sharing the magic of the same luna flame. And no-one knows better than you, the mysterious magic of a full moon.

I rejoice in the singular splendour of our union, but what if we add a cat to the mix? No ominous black cat filled with foreboding, but a mysterious, dream talking tabby. I wonder what it will tell me tonight? For I'm sure it will return. Perhaps its presence will sooth my head, which I must confess is getting worse by the word. Time to stop I think. Hurry home my love, for your little wife, your little Sissy is feeling sad and forlorn. Come home Edgar, come home, and leave me never more.

Yours beloved, beloved yours

Virginia Eliza Clemm Poe... yours.

CATAWALLIN

The stonemasons were restless. The cathedral was only weeks from completion, but the blood debt had yet to be honoured. In the past fifty years they'd been innumerable broken fingers, twenty broken legs, three lost arms and six lost ears. But as yet, there had been no deaths. All the Masons agreed, it had been the safest build any of them could remember; but this created a problem; as divine providence had chosen not to pay the debt for them, they had to do it, someone had to die. Some of the older Masons claimed that the debt would have been paid when the cathedral's foundation stones were laid, but as none of them had been around to see the deed done, no-one could be sure, and a debt is a debt.

'For a stone to be laid, blood must be paid;' the apprentices murmured apprehensively.

'Lest the stone should stray,' their stone-eyed masters muttered.

'It must be a worthy sacrifice,' Bracewell insisted.

'No paid-up members of the guild,' Ackroyd insisted.

'And if the guild member has paid-up, then by rights his apprentice should be protected too,' Brier asserted, 'the apprentice falls under his protection, to do otherwise wouldn't be right.'

'Only if he's any good,' Bracewell snarled, 'we'll have no slackers.'

'And tell me true Bracewell, are not all our lads straight as a plumbline? Are they not all worthy lads?'

The men fell into a truculent silence, for it was true, the apprentices were the best bunch of lads the Masons had ever worked with, and in truth, through their years of long apprenticeship, they'd grown fond of their charges. Not one of them deserved a shove from the spire, or a dropped stone on the back of the neck.

'What if we made it a lesser sacrifice?' Brier ventured.

'For a structure of this size and reverence it has to be worthy,' Bracewell insisted.

The Masons gathered closer, talking in hushed, sharp voices.

'True… true, but what if our predecessors had made an offering, as they should have done when the foundation stones were laid… and we were just making sure, where's the harm?'

'Topping it up, as it were?'

'And what if they didn't? The whole bloody lot will come down.'

'Not if our sacrifice was honest, well intended, and pure of heart … after all, they should have honoured the blood debt when they laid the foundation, and none of us were Master Masons then. None of us were even on site.'

'So it wouldn't be our fault.'

'Indeed, it would not.'

'Agreed.'

'I'm for it. I'll do it,' Ackroyd determined, 'I'll do it tonight.'

Giles Bastet, 9th Heavenly Cat, lord high overseer of accidental death, stretched himself across the cool surface of the white stone, soaking up the sunshine and giving his fur a much needed airing. He'd been jumping between centuries, seasons, weeks and days in order to find the perfect sunning spot for hours, if not minutes; and had finally decided that the gardens of Winchester Abbey in 1107 was the place to be. Yes, there was lots of building work was underway; the clutter of horse's hoofs and clouds of stone dust in the air; but there was also the buzzing of bees, the fussing of flies and the gentle gurgle of the river flowing by. Really, could anything compare to a sunny English afternoon? Such peaceful bliss; and then some bastard caught him by the tail and shoved him into a stinking sack; the bloody cheek of it.

Obviously Giles could have freed himself at any moment, and unleash a whirlwind of retribution, but the thrill of not knowing was exhilarating; Giles decided to wait and see what happened next.

Ackroyd climbed the wooden scaffolding, high into the Cathedrals transepts, and crossed into the rafters of the central tower. Climbing by candlelight he moved cautiously from beam to beam, until he reached a prepared recess in the outer wall. His fingers checked the mound of lime mortar beside his trowel was still moist; and it was. Ackroyd was a Master Mason who knew preparation was everything.

Holding his trowel in his mouth, Ackroyd moved the sack to his lap and traced his hand across the lump within it until he found its head. Taking his trowel in his hand he mouthed a prayer to the great architect, the one true god – and then brought the edge of his trowel down hard across the bulge framed between his hands: once, twice, thrice. The sack was still. He placed it within the recess, and in three minutes had covered the hole with mortar. It ran smooth and true, plush to the wall; if you didn't know it was there, you'd never know it was there. The debt was paid, and the job done.

'Meow.'

Ackroyd nearly fell off the joist. Sitting beside him was a tabby cat with a ragged ear. Exactly like the one he'd just entombed. A moment of doubt gripped his heart. What had been in the sack when he struck it? He hadn't checked its contents before dealing the death blow. And he hadn't looked inside, once the deed was done. So what had he placed in the recess? Certainly not a worthy sacrifice. Ackroyd took his trowel to the wall and removed the mortar, it was still moist enough, he had time to put it right. He pulled out the sack and…how strange; it was empty.

'Come on kitty, here kitty,' he beckoned the cat with twitching fingers, but the cat didn't want to come. Ackroyd searched through his pockets and found a sliver of cheese. 'Come on kitty, come on now, lovely cheese.' The cat approached, nose twitching to scent the cheese. Ackroyd scooped it up with one fluid motion, laid it across his lap and hit it sharply across the neck with his trowel three times. The cat's body went limp. He stuffed the body into the recess and the sack over it; sealing it in with the lime mortar. The finish was smooth, the job complete.

'Meow.'

Ackroyd blanched; the ragged eared tabby was sitting beside him on the beam. How was this possible? He grabbed the cat by the scruff of its neck, held its head against the wall and brought the sharp edge of the trowel down on its neck, four, five, six times. He shoved the bleeding corpse back into the hole, scoped up the lime mortar and pressed it home with both hands. It was moist enough, it would do, perhaps not perfectly smooth but who but spiders would ever see it up close. Job done.

'Meow.'

It couldn't be, he'd almost taken the cat's head off with his trowel. The cat was bewitched; or perhaps it was a different cat. A different cat with the same ragged ear… but it had to be. Ackroyd hacked out the drying mortar with his trowel. The sack was still there, and… the cat was gone… how was this possible… its blood was still on his hands? Ackroyd looked at the cat with terror filled eyes; 'What demon are you to play with me so?'

'What bastard are you, to play with me so?' the cat replied.

Ackroyd jumped to his feet, hit his head on a roof beam, and tumbled forward. He crashed through the plaster ceiling, smashed through the top layer of scaffolding, bounced off the fourth level and fell to the third, which collapsed beneath him, sending him through the second and the first, all the way to the floor of the nave.

Every inch of Ackroyd ached, but wasn't that a good thing? It meant he was alive. It meant his back wasn't broken. He should have broken every bone in his body with such a fall; but the Great Architect looked after his own. He was alive, by God's blessing. He was experiencing God's good grace… it was a miracle! The devil had tried to kill him, but the Great Architect had spared his life.

And then the central tower collapsed into the nave.

Giles Bastet sat on the wall of the cathedral watching the sun come up; it really was an incredible sight from his vantage point. It reminded him of his days watching Ra rise from the peak of the great pyramid, happy days. The old mantra of the old temple makers chimed like a dancing girl's finger-cymbal in his memories; 'for a

stone to be laid, blood must be paid, lest the stones should stray.'
Ah, it was bunkum then, and it was bunkum now; one lesson and
only one lesson rang true, screw with the cats and the cats will screw
with you.

TEXT CAT

@TotalTruthBomb287
Omg did you see what she was wearing??

> @WhiteRite991
> Totally asking for it. She wants cock.

@TotalTruthBomb287
No man. Total dyke #totaltruthbomb

> @WhiteRite991
> So she needs cock to put her right

@TotalTruthBomb287
2 cocks just to be sure

> @WhiteRite991
> Word!

@TotalTruthBomb287
Tag-team the snotty bitch

> @WhiteRite991
> Righteous #judgementman
> #womenknowyourplace

@TotalTruthBomb287
Bitch needs humbling

> @WhiteRite991
> We should do that

@TotalTruthBomb287
Truth. We should film that #manswork

> @WhiteRite991
> In 3D. Close up. Face screaming!
> Send to her parents and her school.

@TotalTruthBomb287
She should be so lucky. She is unworthy of my seed.

@WhiteRite991
Willing to lower myself.

@TotalTruthBomb287
Never to young to learn. Lets do it #totalrush

@WhiteRite991
Roofie party party party

@TotalTruthBomb287
FM whats that?

@WhiteRite991
Wha bro?

@TotalTruthBomb287
Dumb cat trying to get in at my window

@WhiteRite991
You have a cat??????
#totalsurprise

@TotalTruthBomb287
No dude. Not mine. Ugly thing. Ripped up ear. Wants to come in.

@WhiteRite991
Do it. Give it some Spice & film it. SHIT!
You won't believe this.

@TotalTruthBomb287
Wha?

@WhiteRite991
Theres one outside my window 2.
Tabby. His ears ripped up 2.
#amazballs

@TotalTruthBomb287
#coincidence? I say we let them in and do them together

@WhiteRite991
Do it! Burn that pussy

@TotalTruthBomb287
Practise make purr-fect. Letting it in / doing it now

@WhiteRite991
Doing it now. This is gonna be a blast

And the rest is… blessed silence.

THERE, THERE ON THE STAIR

It's true, Giles Bastet, 9th Heavenly Cat, had been to London to visit the queen; and what did he do there? Well, that's an entirely different story and I'm not sure how that first line sneaked into the frame, I can only apologise; it's very disconcerting when stories do this, but there it is, I'm just writing it down. Now, this story is set in Holland, around about 1889 by the looks of things, just on the outskirts of Old Amsterdam, which was called Old Amsterdam even then. The Really Old Amsterdam sank into the sea the same year as Atlantis, but as Really Old Amsterdam was full of neolithic potheads, nobody could write about it.

It's early in the morning, start of the working week and Claus Von Duoff, a fifty-seven-year-old miller, and long-term resident of Old Amsterdam, is feeling the effects of last night's lagers behind his eyes. But the mill's sails need to be set, and the mechanism needs to be checked, because his customers will be arriving soon, and when they do the cogs and dust will be flying all day long.

First job of the day; a quick go-over with a broom. Even the most meticulous miller, and Claus Von Duoff was not one of them, loses a certain amount of flour during the milling process. This spillage settles as a fine dusty sheen over every surface. Although nobody expects a spotless mill, letting that stuff gather is a serious error. If left long enough it tends to clog things up, makes the workspace dangerous; the stairs for example (which are really ladders) are extremely hazardous when coated with a sheen of wholemeal flour, and the stuff is extremely flammable, there are no naked flames in mills, not if you value your life. Spilt grain however is the miller's worst enemy, it's a clarion call to every bandit mouse and rat in a three-mile radius; it's like cocaine to those rodents. Although, as it's part of an actual food group, it's much more necessary than the old Bolivian magic dust.

The reader may have noted that the writer is attempting to interject, indeed force his personality into this tale, in an attempt to emulate the Gonzo style of the late great Hunter S. Thompson, a man who, unlike myself, was overly familiar with Bolivian powder. I am unaware of the late professor's relationship with flour, but I wouldn't put it past him. I on the other hand, have an intimate knowledge of flour and mills, and I'm here to tell you mills are death traps, definitely not the place you'd want to find a minor death related deity, but there he was, a ragged eared tabby cat, right there, there on the stair – which in fact was a ladder.

If there was one thing Claus Von Duoff detested more than mice it was cats – a perverse attitude in a miller – but Claus was a perverse, disagreeable, and dishonest man. His weights and measures were constantly being questioned by his customers, and his habitual practise of adding sweepings and ash to orders was long suspected, and occasionally disputed but – thanks to some swift payments to the relevant authorities - never proven. He was a difficult man to work with, he'd never been able to keep an apprentice for more than six months. They just disappeared and never came back. And when Claus had a hangover embedded behind his eyes, which was most mornings, his questionable personality bordered on the homicidal; and a ragged eared tabby cat sitting on the steps of his mill, was never going to sweeten his mood.

Claus kicked the bottom rung of the rickety ladder, raised a clenched fist and emitted a cannon blast guttural bark at the cat, that made flour fall from the rafters. The cat blinked and held his ground. Claus gripped his broom like a felling-axe and swung at the cat. The broom handle shattered, the ladder shook, and dust flew. The cat yawned.

Something crunched beneath Claus' foot. He looked down to discover the body of a grey mouse. He picked it up by its still limp tail, and shot the cat a furrowed brow; 'fair enough. If you're going to earn your keep you can stay, but stay out of my way.' The cat stood, raised its tail, and leisurely climbed up the ladder, and passed through the hatch to the mill's next level, and out of Claus' sight. Claus tossed the dead mouse into a bucket of sweepings, tightened his apron, and set about his day.

Claus' day did not improve. The mother of his most recent apprentice called in to say her son had left her a note to say he'd run away to join the army. She insisted he was owed a week's pay, and he should give it to her – it was only a pittance but handing out the money set Claus' teeth on edge. The thought of having to train another idiot made his head throb. Having to single handedly haul sacks of grain and flour, up and down the mill's ladders all day long, would make everything else ache. His first customer, Victor Van Dijk, a local bigwig with a contract to supply bread to the parish's alms-houses; arrived with four bags of grain and demanded a discount, as well as his fee being placed on the parish account, this was not good news, as the parish always paid late. The next customer was the Widow De Jong and two of her sons, who arrived with one sack of grain. They disputed the weight of their one single solitary sack for an hour before agreeing a price; and then insisted on bagging it themselves – ruining Claus' chances of contaminating the batch, which reduced his profit margins. Five sacks of grain in one day; it was hardly worth setting the sails, and when he did, Claus discovered that two sail bars had come loose and ripped a two-ell length gash in the sail cloth. It would have to be repaired, yet more expense, yet more lost profit. It was not a good day to be Claus the Miller. So, when the sun dimmed and he finally hauled in the sails and locked off the driveshaft, Claus was ready for several large lagers, and not in the mood to see that damned cat sitting on his folded sacks.

'Get off of there! Get out! Get out. I don't want you in here, out!'

The cat dropped down a step and purred.

Claus grabbed a ball of sacking twine and flung it at the cat, knocking it from its perch. But when Claus stormed across the floor to finish the job, the cat was gone. Raging, he tossed and kicked the sacks this way and that, searching for his prey. 'Meow,' and there it was, on the stair right there on the stair, a little cat with a gloating grin. Claus' grinding teeth ached his gums; and then his face cracked with a jagged grin; he'd had an idea. He retrieved the ball of twine, and the now stiff mouse from the bucket of sweepings and set about his perverse plan.

A noose was tied around the mouse's head, and three ells of twine laid from the steps to the millstone's cogs. Claus positioned himself behind the driveshaft, set the heavy crank lever in place, and prepared to drive the mechanism on by hand. He tugged the twine; just enough to make the mouse dance. The movement caught the cat's eye. Its whiskers twitched. Another tug, and the cat crouched, ready to pounce. Slowly and steadily Claus pulled the twine in, drawing the mouse towards the mill's cogs. The enthralled cat quivered with excitement. The mouse lodged in the teeth of the cog. Claus tugged and the mouse twitched. The cat leapt. Claus drove the crank handle forward. The cogs turned, the teeth bit and the cat screamed. Claus kept the cogs turning – crunch, grind, crunch. When the grinding stopped, Claus reversed the cogs, removed the crank handle, and went to see his handiwork.

The cog's teeth were befouled with blood, fur and unrecognisable mangled matter; it was a mess. But not even the prospect of cleaning up such gore could ruin Claus' mood. His chuckle sounded like grinding glass. He doused the workings with a bucket of water and watched the blood swirl downwards into the millstones, it amused him to think his customers would consume cat tainted bread. He hadn't felt so good in years.

A 'Meeeow,' sounded above him.

Claus looked up to see the ragged eared tabby leering down at him from the third-floor hatch; 'you bastard, how'd you do that?' The cat retreated beyond the hatch. Claus took to the ladder and began to climb.

 The windmill's top floor was hot, cramped, and airless; and given the hour it was also dark. Claus closed the trapdoor behind him, to prevent the cat's escape, and the room's darkness deepened. Claus dropped to his knees, squinted, and crawled along the floorboards with gritted teeth. He'd wring the life out of that cat with his bare hands and rip its stupid head off. His head collided the cog that interlocked with the teeth of the driveshaft, this meant he'd reached the centre of the room without finding the cat, that darned cat was one elusive rat.

'Where are you? You bastard cat!' he yelled, raising a cloud of dust from the floorboards.

And then, just as his mouth and eyes were as full of dust as they could be, the room was illuminated with a beautiful ball of blue light, the clear blue shimmer of a cloudless dawn. If Claus had been more of an esoteric soul, he might have appreciated the beauty of the moment, but seeing as he was in the confines of a windmill's cramped roof space, with a bright blue glowing cat – he was terrified. When the light surrounding the cat changed from blue to flame red, Claus moved into whatever sphincter clenching mode is beyond terrified. When the curved roof above his head ignited, he had exactly half a breath to register his fate, before the entire windmill exploded.

How a minor Egyptian cat deity knew as much about the flammability of free-floating flour escapes me, but I would suggest my own life experience has something to do with it. But what really bothers me is this; why Giles took out Claus Von Duoff at all? He was obviously an arsehole but what real harm did he do? Truth be told, I had no idea until a week after the reported incident, when the local parish dignitaries ordered the wreckage of the windmill to be cleared away and a new mill be put on its foundations. For beneath the wreckage, in the ground beneath the windmill's support struts were found the bodies of three young men; all of which had worked for Claus Von Duoff, one of whom had seemingly written a letter to his mother telling him he was joining the army. That darned cat.

THE CAT IN THE HAT

At the beginning of the day, the gently rising hillside had been an unexceptional fallow field, and then cannonballs pounded it, gouging deep scars into the soft rich earth. By midday repeated cavalry charges and frantic melees had churned the lower ground into a muddy mire, trapping the opposing infantrymen in a bogged down engagement that cost each army dearly. And then came the rain that turned the gentle slope into a mudslide and the muddy plain into a festering sore of confusion. As neither side could carry out an orderly retreat, there was nowhere for either army to go but forward. The death toll was far higher than even the most callous of General's could have predicted; a day poets would recall with biblical allusions, of surpassing slaughter.

As the smoke hung about the field, and the pitiful cries of the dying sank into the befouled soil, one battle raged on, sword against clattering sword, will against will. Captain Willard Fortesque, of the Royal Horse Guards, and Lancer Maurice De Perrin of the Chevaulegere Lanciers, held the field. Both gripped their besmirched leaden sabres in their numb blood smeared hands. Each so desperate to live, they needed the other to die. Both battled the ebb and flow of animal fury and disconsolate desperation that churned within them. Both thinking, 'I'm so tired, please finish me off and be done with it,' whilst neither could find the strength to accomplish the task.

Gripping his sabre with both hands Willard swung desperately at Maurice's head. Seeing the arc of the blade, Maurice stepped backwards, lost his footing, and fell to his knees. His plumed Trojan style helmet lifted from his head and went spinning off into the smoke heavy air. Set off-balance by the power of his mis-stroke Willard's feet slid from under him. He fell face down in the guts of a felled grey stallion. Seeing his chance Maurice jumped to his feet, sank to his shins in the mud, lunged forward and lost his right boot. Unequally unshod, Maurice slid to his right when he meant to go to his left, and toppled backwards into the mud. Not seeing his enemy's predicament for the horse gore in his eyes, Willard slashed blindly at empty air, as his battle to extricate himself from the horse's rank innards, worked him deeper into the bloody mess. Maurice caught his breath, sank his sabre into the earth and tried to pry himself loose. He felt the earth give, heard the slurp of release, gained his feet, and pulled his sabre clear. His enemy's back was before him. Raising his sabre high above his head Maurice threw himself towards his flailing foe. Sensing the Frenchman's attack, Willard swung about to parry the blow; clumsily slashing through Maurice's belly and femoral artery as he did so.

The same look of bewilderment crossed both men's faces, and then Maurice paled, his mouth twitched into a brief smile of relief, and then he was gone. The body of the Lancier collapsed into the dirt at Willard's feet.

Willard stood and surveyed the battlefield, here and there horses were banding together in small clusters, seeking silent comfort amidst the carnage. But all else was stillness, nothing moved but a few fluttering pennants. He turned to his own line but saw nothing but piles of bodies and shattered gun carriages. The French line was just as forlorn. Was there no one left? 'Is there anybody there?' A faint groan sounded somewhere to his left. 'Hello, hello? Can you hear me, speak up!' Two hundred yards away, behind a pile of uniforms a raised hand waved weakly and then fell out of sight. 'Hold on, hold on, I'm coming.' At that moment Willard didn't care if it was a Frenchman, a Pole or a bloody infantryman; it was another soul and he needed to be with them. But quick passage was not possible through the mud; moving quickly was a perilous business, better to move slowly and deliberately, seek out the firmer ground, step over bodies and body parts where you could, and step on them if you had to. It was slow, stomach-churning work; now and then Willard lost his bearings; which pile of bodies was he heading for? There were so many; 'Are you there? Call out man, call out, I'm coming.'

A gloved hand rose above a pile of bodies to his right, wavered, turned to face him, and then walked across the corpses towards him. It stopped at his feet and sat down. A white leather glove with a wagging tabby tail. Willard gripped its forefinger and tossed the glove aside, revealing a ragged eared tabby cat. The cat meowed, brushed a paw across its whiskers and distained to recognise Willard's act of kindness, as only a cat can do. Willard had never been overly fond of cats, he much preferred dogs, but he'd seen too many scavenging mutts on a battlefield to still hold their kind in high regard. But a cat? On a battlefield? Looking for rats perhaps? Rats were always to be found on battlefields, ghastly creatures, always up to grizzly ghastly business; worse than dogs, and yet to see a cat amidst the blood of battle was disconcerting. Nanny Newton's nursery rhyme returned to him; 'Pussycat, pussycat, where have you been? And what have you been up to?' Nanny Newton used to tell him horrid tales of country cats that ate their newly deceased owners – it's probably why he developed his aversion to cats; but that was just one of Nanny's stories wasn't it? There was less truth in it than old pussycat, pussycat going to London to see the Queen; surely?

So how did the glove get stuck on the cat's head? Willard rounded the pile of bodies and there, propped up against them, was the body of Major Douglas Marlborough, of the Royal Horse Guards, his major, and second cousin on his mother's side. A musket ball had taken his right arm off at the shoulder. It lay in his lap, gripped firmly by the Major's gloved left hand, as if he'd meant to have it reconnected later. The detached arm was missing its glove. Willard turned to look for the cat. It was sitting atop the pile of bodies looking down at the fallen major.

'What the hell were you doing puss?' The cat licked its lips and fixed Willard with a contemptuous stare. 'Go on! Get out of it! Go on away with you!' The cat yawned and settled down to watch Willard rant. 'I said get out of here you fiend, go find your dinner elsewhere. Go on, there's rich pickings for sure, but you'll not be feasting on this gentleman, I'm telling you that for nothing.' The cat's whiskers trembled in response, and then its whole body shuddered, as if repulsed at the very suggestion. Such daintiness in such circumstances; the ridiculousness of it pricked Willard's bombast and tickled him pink; he laughed; 'Sorry Puss… have I got that wrong? Here for the rats? Of course you are. But I can't take the risk, you'll have to bugger-off old boy, I can't risk you snacking on a family member now can I?' The cat stared placidly at him but refused to budge. 'Right…' Willard looked at the sabre in his hand and considered his options. 'No there's been enough death here today;' and slipped the blade back into its scabbard. 'You'll have to come with me, pussycat.' Reaching out he plucked the cat from its perch and placed it on his shoulder. Seemingly unsatisfied with this position the cat climbed on top of his head and sat bolt upright like a lookout on a keep, Willard felt its purr tingling his scalp; and then a musket ball from the English lines took off his head.

'Who you firing at Jones?'

'Frenchie Sir.'

'Did you get him?'

'Yes Sir, always Sir, a rifleman never misses.'

'Good shot Jones, but tell me, how could you be sure he was French at this distance?'

'I can tell you more than that Sir, he was a bloody Lancer Sir. It's those bloody Trojan helmets they wear with the puffy plumes. You can see the mugs a mile off even in this smoke.'

'Well… all the same, be careful Jones, wouldn't want you taking out one of our own men by accident.'

'Never happen… oh look at that, coming this way… it's a bloody cat. Shall I shoot it Sir?'

'No Jones, you will not, there's been enough killing for today. Let's see what it wants. Come on pussycat… puss, puss.'

Brenda the Blind sat with her father's goats beneath the shade of an oak tree on the edge of the wood. The goats trusted Brenda and rarely strayed from her reach, and never from the sound of her voice. When she called, the nanny-goats came to be milked, and the kids played with her hair and nibbled her clothes, as she sang them songs of their own mythical heritage. Of all the goats in the village none were as content as those belonging to Brenda's father; all who lived there recognised the truth of it, and valued Brenda for her craft. And this included many of the settlement's other animals; the chickens loved her, the dogs adored her and the cats were devoted as a cat can be. And on this bright crisp morning, as Brenda milked a nanny she called Hazel, a cat called down to them from the branch above her head. Hazel was oddly perplexed and suddenly freed herself from Brenda's hold and started to try and climb the tree, as if to join the cat. Of course, Brenda could only guess at the goat's antics, but knowing her charge, she guessed right; 'Hazel now, come away, you're no cat to go climbing up that tree. Calm yourself. Now then pussycat, if you don't want Hazel up in your tree, you better bring yourself down here to say good morning.' Brenda heard the cats purr before she felt its fur brush against her bare calves.

'There you go, your turn Hazel come on down. All is well. Now let's get to milking, shall we?' And they did, but a questioned remained unanswered for Brenda; who was by nature an inquisitive girl; 'And who be this kitty cat that calls on you Hazel? Is it Bell? Thorn? Old Missy is that you?' Brenda's hand reached out to identify the cat, but her nimble fingers brushed nothing but air. 'Puss cat, where you be pussy cat?' A rough tongue found her milky forefinger and lapped it clean. 'Bold pussy, does that taste good? Here then I can spare you a morsel more.' Cupping her hand into the bucket Brenda held it out to the cat. Feeling it drink, and hearing the pleasure it took in drinking, Brenda deftly slid her other hand over the cat's head; to know it better. 'Who be you then? I don't think I know you…what happened to your ear pussycat? Poor pussycat…' The cat's fur fell away from her touch; 'Puss? Puss? Where'd you go puss, pussycat? Well, what do you think to that Hazel? Comes and drinks and flees, without so much as a bye-your-leave, must be a tomcat that one, no doubt about it indeed.'

Giles Bastet, 9th Heavenly Cat, lord high overseer of accidental death, was enjoying a late breakfast of filleted herring; served to him by a slow, ageing but attentive handmaiden, atop a spray spattered wooden jetty, surrounded by the still waters of a mountain shrouded bay; when all hell broke loose.

Someone shouted, 'Raiders!' and everybody started running around screaming. The women stopped gutting that day's catch, snatched up their children, and fled into the sparse cover of the trees that covered the mountain's lower slopes. Men grabbed battered shields and rusting swords, mallets, boat hooks, sticks, knives and whatever else they could get their hands on; some fled, some stayed; eyes fixed on the two black shapes, shattering the shadows of the bay as they advanced.

'Dragon ships,' the elderly handmaiden rasped, as she plucked Giles from his breakfast and clutched him to her withered breast. Giles reacted to this disrespectful outrage with a spitting hissing fit. The servant immediately regained her senses and returned him to his feet. But the outrage had still occurred; she had touched him! Normally such indecently intrusive acts of blasphemy would reap a claw-fest whirlwind that would shred the perpetrator's thread of life into a thousand gossamer strands, and Giles was ready to do it too! But this usually pious old servant was clearly upset, and he didn't know why; he couldn't stand not knowing why; so Giles decided to let her live, for now at least. But he informed the old crone of his intense displeasure with a whip of his tail; surely a lesson she would not soon forget. But something had disturbed the poor creature's mind; what could possibly make such a devout follower lose her way? Giles needed to know.

'Dragon ships,' the old girl insisted as she reached out for him, 'they'll kill us all kitty.'

Giles hadn't heard the word dragon since his days in the Old Emperor's court, and here he was, thousands of miles and hundreds of years away, hearing that word again. Yes it was actually a different word, a different name, with a whole different set of vowel sounds, but languages come very easily to gods, even minor ones – so he recognised the meaning of dragon. But Giles was perplexed because the Old Emperor would have welcomed a dragon into his palace, and not run away from them like these villagers were doing… what was he missing? Giles swerved out of the babbling servant's reach and turned to observe the cause of his once trusted servant's lack of decorum; he wanted to see this dragon.

But dragon there were none, just two square sailed ships; bows low in the water, decks laden with armed men, cutting through the water side-by-side; the wake of one folding into the wake of the other, as they approached the jetty at tremendous speed.

'Mother Eostre save us,' the blabbering maidservant cried as she fell to her knees, 'the demons of the North.'

Giles was beginning to think he may have to get a new servant, this one was clearly broken. He knew what demons looked like, and they didn't look like hairy monkey men in a boat. And yet, she wasn't alone in her panic, everybody was running away, except for the small group of poorly armed men that was forming on the beach.

A fearful cry and clashing of shields arose from the ships, and then the raiders were upon them; jumping into the shallow waters, boarding the jetty, charging ashore.

'Mother Eostre, save me, save me…' the thin, rag bedraggled body of Giles' maidservant, fell beside him; her head cleaved in two.

Giles looked up to see a grey bladed axe hurtling towards him. He really couldn't be arsed to move. The blade cut him in two, from stem to stern; and on the raider raged. When Giles had half the mind to pull himself together, he viewed the scene with a cold dispassionate eye. The villagers were dead. His maidservant was dead. One or two raiders were dead, and the village was on fire. Anything not killed or burned by the raiders was now being loaded into their boats. By his brief calculations, the raid, and deaths had been worth… four goats, two weeping human children, and the capture of a terrified young woman, Giles knew as Brenda the Blind. There could be no doubt in Giles' mind that the raiders would use Brenda appallingly; there was every chance they already had; but once they discovered Brenda was blind, they would dispose of her. And this seemed to be an awful waste to Giles, the goats liked

Brenda, and Giles liked the goats; goats were funny, with their eyes in the wrong way round; hilarious! Giles launched himself from the jetty and landed beside Brenda and Hazel in the bottom of the boat. Hazel greeted him with a cheery bleat; as an axe wielding hairy man eyed him suspiciously.

As the ships left the bay Giles saw that they were a small contingent of a larger fleet; six ships were at anchor in the shadow of the snow-capped mountain. As the two ships approached, a ship with a red pennant atop its mast called for them to pull alongside.

"Greetings Harald Anderson, and did your deviation bring you riches.'

'No my Jarl, it was poor pickings. It was nothing but a small fishing village, no more than twenty souls.'

'As I see, poor pickings indeed. A few goats, two snot nosed bairns, a weeping girl and her cat. Tell me, how many men did you lose?'

'Two my Jarl, Orm and Toke, old men, slow in the fight.'

'Slow in the fight, but quick of wit. Unlike you, Harald Anderson. Because of your actions, word of our presence is now travelling along the coast. What could and should have been ours will now flee, or prepare for our arrival. Two good men are dead, and more will die… for a few goats and a weeping girl… and your pride.'

'My Jarl!'

'Your ship is now the tail. You'll have no more bounty in this season. And in case you haven't noticed… that girl is blind. Deal with it.'

The men of the ship glared at Harald, muttering oaths under their beards, as they busied themselves with rope and sail. Harald was not unaware or unaffected. He stormed from the bow of the ship to the deck where the girl lay with her arm around a nanny-goat, brandishing his sword before him. The girl did not shrink away, Jarl Svenson was right, the girl was blind. Harald grabbed the girl by the hair and immediately found himself sitting back in the bow of the ship, with an ache in his guts and stars before his eyes. Hazel the goat bleated her defiance; these hairy humans might have separated her from her kid, but they would not lay a hand on her milkmaid.

The men of the boat roared with laughter at Harald's felling; stirring Harald's embarrassment into a fierce rage. He was on his feet, sword raised, bearing down on the girl; when another blade blocked his path.

'Calm yourself Harald Anderson, she is protected by an old god, I would not try again,' it was Frode Runeson, and had it been any other, Harald would have run him through, but Frode was the son of a wisewoman that many believed to be a witch, and so had to be heard; if not contended with, 'heed me, no good will come of it.'

'It's a goat, and a blind goat herd, and no more.'

Frode pulled Harald close to him and whispered in his ear, 'I do not mean the goat.'

'The girl is no god.'

'Nor does she claim to be, look…' Frode pointed to the tabby cat that sat in the girl's lap, looking for all the world as if it was watching birds at play. 'I killed that cat this morning. I struck it in two. And yet, here it is whole.'

'Frode, one cat can look like another. A tomcat can resemble a mother or its own father. There is no mystery to this.'

'Aye this is true, but how many cats have that ragged ear? The one I killed did, I am certain… and yet it is whole again. That is not a cat my liege. As a boy I travelled with my father to trade with the land of the East, where their gods are carved in stone and formed into weirding animal forms; eagles, jackals and the cat is not the least of these. They call her Bastet, beware my liege, she sees all and protects that girl through that cat.'

Harald sheathed his sword and turned his back on the cat, lest its evil eye claim his soul. He would have to find another way of carrying out his Jarl's command. Or perhaps, somehow, he could transfer the curse to his master's vessel and change his own fortune for the better.

That night the fleet anchored in a sheltered fjord that concealed their ships from all but passing crows. Many men chose to stay on their ships, but others took to the land and built fires to tell tales around, and warm their weary bones. Harald sought out his Jarl's fire and presented himself with a bowed contrite head.

'My Jarl, your words were wise and my actions rash. I only meant to bring you honour…'

'And instead, you bring me a goat and a blind girl.'

'This is true,' and it was literally true, because he had brought both bound girl and goat with him to the fire, 'but she is more than a blind goatherd my Jarl, she is a storyteller. I found her singing songs to her goats, calling them by name and weaving histories for them that they could never have known. I tell you she is a storyteller like no other.'

'But she cannot know of the tales of Thor and Odin, so what use…'

'Yes I do,' Brenda declared, 'I have known the story of Thor and Freya since my youth. My mother was named Liv, which in your tongue means shelter. She was my shelter and my rock, and my teacher.'

Jarl Svenson, smiled and made space by his fire for young Harald Anderson; 'Come then, let us hear the goatherd's song, it will help pass the hour if nothing more.'

Giles Bastet was bemused, baffled even. He'd been sure the hairy brute monkeys were going to kill the girl and eat the goat; or vice versa; and here they were listening to her sing! And enjoying every minute of it by the looks of things. This was very peculiar monkey business indeed; first they kill, rape and raze his servant's village to the ground; and then they're welcoming his blind servant and demanding from her a song?! How was this normal behaviour, even for a monkey? What was wrong with these people?

If Giles had not been so distracted, he might have seen Frode Runeson approaching him with a sack. As it was, finding himself back in a sack, being carried to who knows where; was oddly reassuring. It looked like things were back to normal at last; all Giles had to do was find out what was going to happen next; and a sack is a great place for that.

Hazel bleated forlornly and Brenda responded by feeling for her teats. She still had milk, but now that she'd been separated from her kid, it wouldn't be long before they dried up. And then what would they do with poor Hazel? Did Svenson's raiders have wit enough to take them both back to their homeland, or would they just eat her? Brenda may have proved her worth as a storyteller, but she could not guarantee the safety of her fractious goat. And what of the cat? That odd ragged eared cat, what had become of him? She'd spent hours onboard Jarl Svenson's ship worrying about that cat, searching for him everywhere, annoying all the crewmen, and then suddenly there he was, back on her lap, purring fit to burst. And the ship wasn't a happy ship anymore. Yes, they continued to raid and maraud with a great deal of zeal and much abandon. But the trouble was their reputation went before them and so little resistance was offered; and little was gained. And then there were the series of accidents that befell Jarl Svenson's ship, unsettling his crew. Little things at first, splinters through toes, heads cracked by the beam, an oar in the groin, a lone wasp in the eye. Minor, piffling things. But it did seem that all those struck by these minor piffling woes, would soon take a turn for the worse. Three had fallen overboard, one had fallen on his sword, and another who swallowed a fish hook had to be finished off by Jarl Svenson himself. The crew were not happy. The men were talking about a curse. But they could not make up their minds, was she to blame or the goat?

It seemed to Giles that 'next', was more of the same; and that was an issue. He'd awoken in a different boat, beside dear Hazel, who sat alongside sweet Brenda; and that was as far as the 'next' took him. The raiders just kept on going, doing what they did and Giles, being what he was, had to carry on doing what he did. He could be no other, he had to be what he was. It was a shame really. He didn't have anything against the men on the ship. He could tolerate them; they were treating his goat and his servant well; so he was willing to put up with their wrong hairiness and their smells... but he was the lord high overseer of accidental death; what was he supposed to do? Deny himself?

'My crew is depleted, I must have more men,' Jarl Svenson declared as he stood before the campfire. His answer was silence. 'I want men for my oars.'

'The men fear to sail with you Jarl Svenson,' spoke Frode Runeson, 'for your ship is cursed.'

'Who says so?'

'You've lost more men than all others combined my liege. The men will not sail with you,' Harald insisted.

'Will you sail with me Harald?'

'Not I Jarl, not while the witch lives.'

'The witch? You mean the storyteller? The blind girl I told you to slay, that you gifted to me. What is your game Harald Anderson?'

'No Jarl, I do not mean the girl. By my troth, Brenda of the tales is a blessing to us all, long may she serve at your court. I mean the cat.'

Jarl Svenson had heard some odd stories in his time. It was part of being a Viking; you grew up with strange tales, most of which you believed, until you didn't, but a witch cat? He had never believed in that, and he wasn't about to start; 'there is no witch cat, it's just a cat.'

'It's a living curse my Jarl,' Frode Runeson declared, 'a foreign god in our land.'

'A god? A god now is it. A moment ago, it was a witch, and now it's a god. Be careful, or by the end of the day the sky won't be big enough to contain yon cat.'

'It's a devil!' Sven Thalson cried, taking to his feet. 'All through the voyage, time and time again, the blind girl searches for it, and makes us search for it too; but it can't be found. And then, there it is on her lap. It's a devil and she's a witch.'

'She's a blind girl and you're all fools. But if it brings you peace. I will deal with your cat god and be done with it. But if any of you harm a hair on that girl's head, you'll answer to my sword. And then I want oarsmen.'

A grumble of agreement rounded the campfire, and Jarl Svenson knew there would be no peace until the deed was done.

Giles Bastet, waited on the ship. He saw the flaming torches of the men approaching and knew what was to come. He was to be killed and the deed needed to be seen to be done. So be it. He was ready to play his part. Jarl Svenson boarded the ship, sighted the cat sitting beside the masthead, and stepped down onto the deck. He strode towards the cat, axe raised, teeth clenched in grim determination. He swung at its head. The cat stepped backwards; Svenson missed. He swung again, this time downwards to smite the cat in two; his axe lodged in the boards of the hull. Cursing in fury, Svenson raised his axe high above his head and… the axe head dislodged from the handle and clattered to the deck behind him. Svenson drew his knife and slashed at the cat. The blade seemed to pass through the cat's body, leaving it purring and intact. The men on the shore grew agitated and panicked, prayers were said and oaths to Odin reaffirmed. Svenson grabbed a shield and threw it at the cat. The cat ducked. The shield smashed the helm of the ship's rudder.

'Demon Cat!' Svenson cried, drawing his sword.

Giles had never been so insulted; demon indeed! He let the swing of the sword pass through his whiskers once more; and then it was his turn. Svenson's blade cut through the rope that fixed the ship's single beam upright to the mast. The beam dropped. As Svenson stepped backwards to avoid the beam, his heel caught the edge of his fallen axe head, cutting his Achilles tendon in two. Svenson's leg folded beneath him, sending him sprawling across the deck. Svenson tried to regain his footing, but his leg would not obey. A frantic bleating came from across the water; Svenson looked up, just in time to see Hazel the goat leaping from the adjoining ship. Goat's head met the man's head; and there could only be one victor.

'Hazel you sweet thing, you really shouldn't have, I had it all under control,' Giles purred.

'Fire! By Odin's blood bring them down! Burn the devils!'

A rain of torches and flaming arrows followed. And so, the ship drifted out to sea, carrying the burning body of a great war chief, a goat and a demon cat with it.

In the years to come, Brenda told the story so many times, she had to change it to keep it interesting for herself, but still, by the time she was an old lady, the tradition of the burning boat was well-established. And King Harald's line did all it could to shape the tale that led to his hegemony. Giles of course moved on, his time with Hazel in the land we now call Morocco was short by divine standards, but sweet none-the-less. And Hazel's offspring can be seen there still; climbing trees as really, only a cat should.

WORSE THINGS… FILM SHORT

FADE IN.

EXT. OPEN SEA. NIGHT.

Establishing Shot; Moonlight on water. CUT TO; MAN treading water. CLOSE-UP: the MAN's face. Panting. Exhausted. Water lapping at his face. He struggles to set himself onto his back. Does so. Looks up into the cold indifferent moonlit night.

CUT TO FLASHBACK: EXT. DAY.

An overcrowded refugee boat. Rapid montage of terrified faces. Men, woman, children shouting and screaming. The MAN stands on the bow of the boat holding a machine gun on the people. He is shouting, snarling but his words are lost in the screams. He is ordering people into the water. At his feet a young woman cowers. She tries to re-join the main group but the man strikes her on the head with the gun barrel, knocking her down. He intends to keep her and force the others off the boat. She tries to crawl to the main group, the MAN kicks her and stands over her, claiming her as his own. He levels the gun at the other refugees; and screams a command. They edge towards the side of the boat – it rocks. The girl kicks and screams out in panic. The MAN reaches down and grabs her arm and pulls her up. Another woman jumps forward and grabs her. A moment of struggle, the boat rocks more wildly. The MAN loses his grip, steps backwards, trips and falls off the boat.

CUT TO: EXT. OPEN SEA. NIGHT.

Moonlight on water. The MAN is floating on his back. CLOSE UP: He is falling asleep. He slips under the water. The surface of the water stills – seconds later a thrashing of water and panic as he comes up gasping for breath. He tries to set himself onto his back but can't. He hears a slight knocking as something approaches in the darkness. He peers into the darkness. Moonlight on water.

MAN'S POV: A tabby cat floating on a floating pile of trash washes itself as it floats towards the MAN. The MAN is amazed and relieved. CLOSE UP: MAN'S face. We see hope. He can claim the cat's trash island and survive. He tries to swim towards it. The cat jumps from the trash into the water and disappears. The trash is dispersed by the MAN'S frantic thrashing. CLOSE UP: The man weeps, pants – sudden sharp pain, as the wet cat climbs from his back to the top of his head and starts washing. The MAN tries to swat the cat away. The cat digs in its claws. CLOSE UP: Of the Tabby cat, we see its ragged right ear, as it settles down to wash. The cat looks up at the stars. We hear the MAN, gasping, bubbling, drowning as the image of the cat sinks down out of frame – the cat yawns as it drops out of shot.

EXT. NIGHT. OPEN SEA. A still moonlit sea.

BLACKOUT. END.

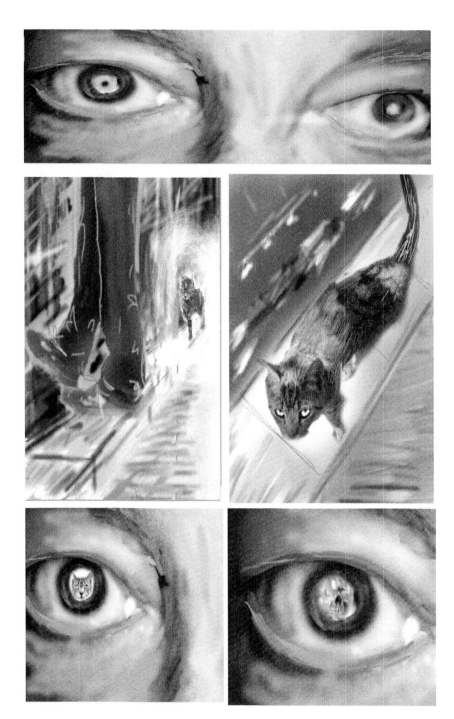

SNOW CAT

An expanse of wind blasted snow shimmers in the heatless sun. Two figures, bulky stumbling bundles, force their way through the thigh-high snow. If they can make it to the safety of the treeline, they may have a chance; their tracks will be lost in the forest and the Gulag's guards may give up and leave them to the mercy of the wolves. Love brought them together, desperation drove them to escape, hope spurs them on. But the treeline is a long way away; and Sven already has a bead on them.

Sven feels the iron hard earth beneath his feet, crouches into the snow, presses the butt of his M1891 into his shoulder, and fixes his sight on the leading grey bundle. Sven's breath streams from his lips. The weight of the trigger beneath his finger gives – the sky cracks and the first bundle falls. The second bundle freezes. Sven likes it when they run. This is too easy no fun at all. But the bundle won't run. It just stands there frozen in the frozen landscape – it's too easy, but he has a job to do. Sven takes the shot – the sky cracks and the bundle collapses in on itself.

Sven tucks his M1891 back into its blanket, replaces his glove, and begins to retrace his steps through the snow. A cry breaks the silence. Impossible, it was a kill shot, he felt it, he saw it. The cry becomes a shriek, no - a wail. The unmistakable high-pitched wail of an infant.

What to do? There's only three hours of daylight left, and it's a stone-cold three-hour trudge back to the compound; best to get going. But Sven knows that wail will attract the wolves, and he doesn't want to contend with them. Sven unwraps his rifle and levels the sight on the kill. Nothing to be seen, nothing to shoot at; Sven spits and heads towards the kill.

Sven stands above the bundle, examining his handiwork. A perfect shot. Dead centre, the spray of blood a perfect scarlet fan in the snow. If the shot had been another inch to the left it would have taken-out the squirming lump on the bundle's back. If he'd known he could have made that shot for sure, two for one. But there it is squirming and wailing to the cold indifferent world. What to do?

What he always has to do, the dirty work that has to be done. A bullet would obliterate it, and he really doesn't want that picture in his head. Sven felt the hilt of his knife beneath his palm – but a skewered babe was another picture he didn't need in his head. So, it was boot or rifle butt, ugly choices, a dirty job.

Sven has an idea, he grabs hold of the bloody bundle and turns it onto its back, face up, squirming lump down into the snow. The cry is instantly muffled but not silenced, but it won't take long. It will fall into silence wrapped in the dwindling warmth and scent of its mother's body, a mercy really. Sven examines the woman's face. A young mother, younger than he'd expected, her face not yet hardened by life in the camp. How had she kept her condition hidden? What was she thinking? She could have handed the child in; the state would have taken care of it. But to run into the wilderness with a child, what did she think was going to happen? It was him or the wolves, it was a mercy really, he wasn't to blame.

A shadow jumps across the surface of the snow, Sven's heart leaps and the knife jumps into his hand. A small, snow sprinkled cat sits on top of the first felled bundle licking its paw. A town cat, a tabby cat with a ragged ear – food. Just like everyone else Sven had eaten cats and dogs during the siege, many preferred the taste of dog, but Sven had developed a taste for spit-roasted cat flesh. An unexpected treat indeed.

Sven sheathed his knife, pulled the glove from his hand, and dropped the rifle's blanket to the snow. All he had to do was take off its head – an easy shot. He pressed the butt into his shoulder and took aim. His breath streamed from his lips; his finger tightened, and the sky cracked. The bullet smashed into his shoulder and threw him backwards, embedding him deep into the snow. Flames of fire and ice raged through his body; his shoulder was smashed, the arm limp and useless. But how? The bullet had ricocheted; impossible.

The tabby cat with the torn ear seemed to glide over the snow and sniffed at the still, now silent second bundle. Arching its back, fur raised like daggers it turned to Sven and hissed. Sven reached across his body and pulled his knife from its sheath. The cat spat, sat back on its haunches, raised its head and howled.

In the distance, the howl was answered. The cat returned the call. Sven threw himself forward, slashing wildly at a blue flash. The cat was gone. In the distance, howls sounded, the wolves were coming.

GILES BASTET & THE CIRCLES OF HELL.

It was spring and Giles Bastet, 9th Heavenly Cat, lord high overseer of accidental death, son of Holy Bastet, Goddess of Protection, felt the fundamental urges of creation flowing through him – which was bad news for some poor sap. For Giles needed more than just a coincidental, humdrum accident to sooth his passion. He needed something big, mayhem and destruction on a monumental scale… so what the hell was he doing in Basingstoke?

Basingstoke of all places; of all the possible places in the infinity of time and space; he was in Basingstoke. It just wouldn't do! Giles licked the back of his front left paw and rubbed it along the bridge of his nose. Instantly the air around him fizzed and sparkled as a ball of blue light swallowed him whole, and spat him across the universe, to deliver him to… the grey concrete blocks of Basingstoke's multi storey car park. Well, that had never happened before. Giles was intrigued, and for the sake of enquiry he tried again – fizzle, spark. As the ball of blue infinity pulled him out of time and space, Giles set his catty pre-pounce focus on the shining streets of Belle Epoque Paris 1898 and leapt towards it; to find himself deposited in… the shining commercial district of Basingstoke's business park. There it was then; he was clearly meant to be there – it was that or the gravitational pull of the town's surfeit of roundabouts was messing with his immutable powers. But if here? Why now? Perhaps that was the issue, time… but what is time but a catnip toy on a string. Let's batter the hell out of it and start at the beginning – fizzle, spark, blue light, pop.

A wooded clearing surrounded by the thick green foliage and layered shadows of a verdant, ancient woodland. Lush, deep pile lichens covered the twisted roots of sky-scraping trees that rose, silvered and shining, from rich mouldering leaf littered soil, enriching the air with a soup of scents; life and life triumphant.

A giant tan coloured cat with bread knife sized fangs, stepped from the shadows and eyed Giles cautiously.

'Well, if it isn't, Great, great, great, great, great… oh why bother?' Giles huffed. 'Don't get any ideas Granddad, I'm not hanging around.'

The sound of something approaching through the foliage alerted the giant cat. It sank to its haunches ready to pounce. Seconds later, three mud bespattered men battled their way into the clearing and froze in terror at the sight of the crouching cat. In an instant the cat did the maths, weighed-up its odds and fled back into the forest. The men laughed, fell to their knees panting, holding their hands to their chests, unable to believe their luck.

'Oh you bastards,' Giles hissed.

The men looked to one another and then to Giles. A flint tipped spear was slowly raised and reached out towards Giles. Giles took a step backwards. The man with the spear stepped forward, and planted his foot on the tail of a sleeping porcupine hidden in the deep leaf litter. As he grabbed his foot with both hands his spear fell from his grasp and lodged in a knot of roots. Not wanting to lose the valuable spearhead the hunter grabbed for the spear's shaft, lost his balance, fell to the ground, snapping the shaft in two. The porcupine, alarmed by being so rudely roused from its slumber, charged backwards, impaling the man's face and throat with a hundred needle sharp barbs. Seeing their brother's plight, the two men rushed to his aid. One caught his foot in a root, stumbled forward and impaled himself on the broken spear shaft. The other rushed at the porcupine, flint axe raised – the porcupine raised its quills – shredding the man's hand and wrist as it plunged towards it. All three men screamed. The sabre-toothed cat, recognising the sound of terror, returned.

'Now you see… that all makes sense to me now. Over to you Grandad,' Giles yawned, stretching a paw – as he fizzled into the future.

Giles arrived on the edge of a tilled field, surrounded by thick silver birch woods. At one end of the field a small group of men felled trees, whilst others trimmed the lumber and fed the spoils into a large fire. Another group of men busied themselves splitting the trimmed logs into stakes, whilst three men and a harnessed horse, walked the field, driving the stakes into the ground. Watching over this industry was another man on a horse, with a large, sheathed sword hanging at its flank.

Giles was confused by horses. A confusion that had often boiled into frustrated contempt. They were his servant's servants, and yet they had the strength, power, and spirit to dethrone their rulers and stamp him into the dirt. But they didn't do it? For the price of a bale of hay and an apple, they carried man around on their backs and carried all his burdens. They even carried him into many of his battles... a deeply flawed animal was a horse. And yet, Giles couldn't deny they were beautiful in their own way, and could be very peaceful company.

'Greetings horse,' Giles mumbled beneath his purr; a language superior horses are known to understand.

The horse pulled against its reins, lowered its head in respect and huffed. A greeting generally recognised as, 'Greetings god cat, peace be with you.'

'Still got a monkey on your back then? Why do you put up with it?'

'It is the noble path of service.'

'No... its servitude.'

'You are blind to the truth god cat.'

'Yes, I know, you've told me before. I've heard it from your kind a thousand times. But you'll observe... I am the god, you are the horse... with a heavy talking ape on your back.'

'I beg to differ.'

'And as always, noble horse, I shall allow it. So what's this ape up to?'

'Lord Basing is staking out his land.'

'His land. How very ape. This is mine because I say it's mine. And it's his because he's the one with the sword and the big horse that doesn't know any better. Don't you remember what it was like roaming around wherever you liked, wherever you willed without boundary or halter, when all this just was as it was, and belonged to no one?'

'No.'

'You're a bloody liar. Has your Lord Basing got a son?'

'Yes, he has god cat, why do you ask?'

'Because I'm about to make him an orphan.'

Fizzle, blue light and flash – Lord Basing's horse reared up in fright, throwing rider from his seat and onto the point of a newly trimmed stake.

A muddy field, surrounded by more muddy fields, filled with fighting, screaming, dying men. Defenders of a high brick wall fought others who tried to storm their wall; all willing to die for the sake of a wall.

'Nest of Romanists!'

'No quarter!'

'And none given!'

And on the armoured apes fought, filling the sky with smoke and their cries. Giles had seen it all so many times before, a confounding bore. Best let the monkeys tear themselves apart and move on – fiz, spark, buzz and flit, into the blue tomorrow.

Giles sat on the concrete wall of the concrete carpark looking down on the concrete town it surrounded. Outside the wall, the shining towers of commerce reached for the sky, beyond them, ran interwoven black rivers of tarmac, and created islands of shelter, dwellings men called homes, where Giles knew many of his clan slept and fed, worshipped by their own monkey servants. The noise and smell of traffic had infused everything; Giles could feel it invading his fur, and he thought of the scent of the forest that was there before, and the snarl of the sabre-toothed cat. He wondered if mankind was aware of the toll it took on the world? Were they determined to bring about their own end, by ruining the world? Would it be a deliberate act or an accident? And if so, as the god of accidental death, was he obliged to stop them?

Six stories below, a man in a leather jacket, finished eating his burger, crumpled the paper wrapping into a ball and threw it to the ground. Searching his pockets for some gum, he tossed sweet wrappers, ticket stubs, and tissues to the ground. Six stories up, a suddenly discombobulated porcupine charged backwards away from the preening tabby cat that sat on the edge of the concrete wall, and found himself falling towards…

GILES BASTET & THE CAT

Giles Bastet, 9th Heavenly Cat, lord high overseer of accidental death, rarely thought of his tail, why would he? it was just there and had always been there. He couldn't remember when he'd stopped being fascinated by its presence, but at some point in divine time his tail had stopped being an object of fascination and was just… there. And yet, the inner conviction that 'it' was another; that is, a different entity to himself, remained; as his mother the Great Holy Goddess Bastet (Blessed be her name) was fond of saying; 'I am a cat but my tail is another.' It was like having a flag of intent attached to his rear end, unfortunately Giles didn't always agree with the messages it was sending. And today was such a day, here he was, relaxed, warm, comfortable and well-fed on a balmy afternoon in high summer and his daft tail was wafting about declaring war on all who passed – it was annoying, and a little unnerving, because Giles had to admit, the tail was often right.

Giles looked down the massed sails and rigging to the ship's deck far below, and saw a shadow he didn't much like the look of, possibly a rat but if it was, it was a big one, perhaps it was a monkey? The ship's crew had stayed on the island for over a week with the ship anchored in the bay, and they often brought back animal oddities after their layovers. Tortoises, disgusting parrots and once a nanny goat and kid, which Giles had taken rather a shine to. But alas after two weeks at sea the kid died, and the poor nanny-goat pined, weakened, and her milk ran dry. So the crew ate them both. Giles stubbornly snubbed the crews offering to him, to mark his disapproval. Rats often got onboard during these layovers, especially in the bigger ports. Giles didn't mind, he let them get on, the more the merrier, it was a fresh larder as far as he was concerned. Giles saw it again, a dark shape circling the base of the mizzen mast. Giles' hackles rose; and then a crew member, dropped to his knees before the shape and petted it. Giles was out of the crow's nest, down the mast, over the yardarm, along the shroud and down the ratline before the ship hit the next wave.

'Lookie here, tabbies got some competition,' the kneeling crewman called out to his brothers-in-arms.

'Get back to your post Hobbs or it's a different cat you'll be tasting, one with nine tails.'

Giles had heard of this strange cat with nine tails many times since being on board HMS Intrepid, but despite looking from stem to stern and crow's nest to orlop, he'd never found the beast. Seafaring men the world over loved their tall tales of huge catches and strange beasts.... And yet when they had an actual deity sitting in their rigging, they failed to honour him, and made him hunt for his own food... or offered him goat.

'There's only room on this ship for one cat, one of them will have to go.'

Giles' tail nearly threw him sideways on hearing this, the monkeys were becoming restless.

'No Sir, please, that would bring us nothing but bad luck.'

Too bloody right it would – he'd skin the lot of them.

'Bad luck? If a black cat isn't a bad omen tell me what is?'

Giles couldn't agree more.

'He's not black Captain, look, the tip of his tail's as white as snow.'

Giles felt a furball jump in his stomach, it couldn't be, could it? Giles felt the tug of his tail and looked back to see it dancing with a ferocity that should have detached it from its moorings. The tail knew, and the tail was seldom wrong. Giles jumped up into the rigging, climbed to the mizzen's topsail and meowed loudly at the preening cat below. The cat ceased its ablutions, looked up into the rigging and followed on a pace.

'Giles is that you?'

'You know full well it's me, and I'd thank you to greet me in the correct manner, according to tradition.'

'Really...?'

'You greeted me, so it's your duty.'

'You meowed first... oh very well then, if I must...' the black cat straightened its neck and pricked up its ears in salute, 'Greetings Giles Bastet, 9th heavenly cat, son of Holy Bastet, lord overseer of... what was it?'

'You know damn well, damn you,' Giles spat.

'But do I? Oh yes, of course... overseer of accidental death. I greet you.'

Giles puffed up his fur, straightened his back, pushed his neck up until it ached, and pointed his ears - ragged and otherwise - to his mother in the sky; 'greetings Fred Bastet, 8th heavenly cat, son of Holy Bastet, lord overseer of spite. I greet you, brother.'

'Brother, and how are you Giles? Lord of the clumsy…' Fred stretched out on the beam and tucked his paws under himself, 'seen mother?'

'Of course I haven't seen mother. What are you doing here Fred?'

'Doing? What do you think I'm doing, I'm being me and spreading spite. And having a rare old time of it I must say.'

'What spite could you possibly have been spreading on that island?' Giles' whiskers fluttered dismissively.

'Careful now brother, you know what happened last time you questioned my purpose.'

Giles felt a sting in his ragged ear; he would never forget his brother's spite, 'Answer the question will you… call it professional curiosity.'

'Curiosity, who can deny curiosity? It's rather simple really, I arrived on the island three weeks ago on a trading vessel. The ship's humans wanted freshwater and women and were willing to trade for cloth. The islanders were willing to trade water but not their women. So the sailors made sure the rolls of cloth they traded were riddled with mildew and rotten to their core. Ten of the islanders have died from just unrolling the stuff. So, in spiteful return, these water barrels the islanders traded with this bunch of bow legged monkeys, are laced with urine and the blood of a not entirely healthy turtle. I thought I'd come along and watch the fun.' Fred closed his eyes and purred with satisfaction.

Giles felt his tail bristle, 'Is that really spite? Isn't that just bad business? If the sailors get sick and discover the trick, they'll come back and kill all the islanders.'

'…out of spite,' Fred Bastet's purr dropped to a pitch that cats the world over recognised as the sublime purr, indicating a state of deep satisfaction.

'I don't know… that's the trouble with spite. It's such a nebulous calling.'

'Nebulous,' Fred Bastet's eyes sprung open, 'what could be more nebulous than an accident. The very term indicates a haphazard event. They happen all over the world without your blessing thanks to these… idiot monkeys. What on earth is wrong with your tail Giles? Do you have worms?'

Giles looked to see that his tail was rotating like a windmill's sail, 'Ignore it… it's been doing that all day.'

'Imagine that, immortal intestinal worms, worms from here to eternity… wormholes in time and space.'

Able Seaman Able Jones, leant out from the mainsail's arm and spat tobacco juice down onto the head of Ordinary Seaman Walice, who was scrubbing down the quarterdeck.

'I do not have worms.'

Ordinary Seaman Walice, who had a severe aversion to seagulls immediately jumped to his feet and blindly hurled his wooden deck brush skyward, hitting Seamen Belcher squarely in the forehead, knocking him from his hold on the mizen royal, sending him plummeting down to the quarterdeck; where he landed on top of Captain Fitzroy-Gibbons, killing both men instantly.

'If you say so brother…' Fred inspected the flapping tail intently, 'in that case something must be worrying you… you've not been neutered have you Giles?'

Carpenter John Turney was attending to a splintered bulwark on the fo'c'sle when he had the overpower urge to stick the splinter into the bowed backside of Able Seamen Stainton. Thinking himself stung by some poisonous tropical insect, he rolled across the deck kicking and screaming. One kick sent Able Seamen Belcher overboard, where the weight of his carpenter's chisels sent him straight to the bottom; and another kick, nicked Seamen Balls left bollock, causing him to tumble from the fo'c'sle to the main deck, where he collided with Seamen Trigg; who was instructing the young Hand Thatcher, in the art of cannonry. Unfortunately, the unexpected arrival of Seamen Balls, caused Trigg to drop a 6lb cannon ball on Thatcher's left foot; instantly turning Thatcher's perfectly good foot into mush.

'No, I have not been neutered Fred, I would kindly ask you to mind your own business.'

Fred batted Giles' tail with the back of his paw, 'well somethings bothering it, you know what mother used to say, I am cat but…'

Thatcher's piteous scream so disturbed Ship's Surgeon Mellows, below deck in the medical bay, that instead of lancing the boil on Able Seamen Johnson's groin, he severed Johnson's member, and two of his own fingers. Understandably perturbed by this most callous of cuts, the no-longer able, Able Seaman Johnson hit Surgeon Mellows across the head with a lit lantern; killing Mellows outright, and dousing Johnson and the deck in flame.

'Yes, I know what mother used to say, thank you very much.'

The cry of 'Fire!' was heard across the ship. The crew looked to the quarterdeck and saw the felled body of Captain Fitzroy-Gibbons. Panic ensued, someone shouted, 'All hands on deck!' and someone else shouted, 'We're being boarded!' Cutlasses were called for, and the arms store broken into – necessitating the murder of Able Seamen Richards; who had been given the task of guarding the arms room that very morning. He died doing his duty, but this made having his throat throttled none the less painful.

'Really Giles, why so tense. Anybody would think you're not pleased to see me.'

Seamen Forbes thought Seamen Fibbs had a better cutlass than him, and so, believing himself to be the better swordsmen, snatched it from his hand. Fibbs, being a cutpurse who'd been press-ganged into service, and had promised himself he'd never be taken advantage of again; always carried a small dagger, lest the need to use it should arise; and as it had arisen, he used it to cut Forbes' belly.

'Pleased to see you… of course I'm not pleased to see you.'

Seeing the spray of Forbes' blood, the desperate men thought themselves engaged in close quarter combat, 'Repel all borders!' was called, and 'Give no quarter!' and so, set about cutting one another to pieces.

'You're not?' Fred purred, 'oh I'm heartbroken, truly I am, that my own dear brother should reject me.'

First Mate Edwin Tagg rose from his cabin and ran towards the sounds of battle. Seeing none but his own crew in the throng, he thought them caught in the act of mutiny, and demanded order, but none came. His pistol was always loaded and ready. He aimed into the throng of thrashing men and fired.

'I'm not rejecting you Fred, I just can't stand the sight of you.'

The lead shot shattered Fibbs head, broke the nose of Apprentice Carpenter Calum Cock and took out the eye of Ordinary Hand Roger Fiddle, who up until that point had been the prettiest boy on the ship; a fact he made the most of, as best he could.

'Well, there's nice... I suppose I'm a fool for expecting better from such a minor deity; what was it again Overseer of the Bumbling Clumsy?'

Grief-stricken by his sudden loss of beauty, maddened by the fury of war and enraged by the turmoil pressing in on him from all sides; Fiddle lost his shit. He cut, bit, gouged his way towards the hand that held the quivering pistol; a demon's scream and a curse upon his bloody tongue.

'Accidental Death!'

Seeing the menace and malice in Fiddle's one eye, Tagg turned on his heels and fled for the captain's cabin. If the captain wasn't there, Tagg knew where he kept his own stock of ball and charge.

'Coincidental 'is more like... no wonder mother never talks about you, she must be ashamed. You know, by rights, the runt of the litter should be eaten by the mother to keep up her strength... but no, not our merciful mother, she spared the weakest of the litter. She must rue the day. Is it really any wonder the house of Bastet has fallen out of favour?'

Tagg reached the captain's cabin to find Seamen Thomas, Jones and Evans – collectively known as the Welsh Boys – laying the captain's body out on his desk. Being a jingoist with no respect for national identities, Tagg thought the worst of the Welsh Boys and charged them; empty pistol raised above his head. The Welsh Boys immediately knocked him to the floor, kicked him to death and began ransacking the captain's belongings.

'I have ended civilisations, brought down empires, ended dynasties, what have you done Fred? Got the servants to piss into barrels. Mother would be so proud!'

Ordinary Hand Roger Fiddle, due to the loss of his eye, the pain of his affliction, the anguish of his defilement, and the sorrow of all the lost attention he would never know, lost his quarry, lost his way and lost all hope. He finally found himself standing on the orlop, lowest deck of the ship; where he now belonged, lowest of the low. Before him the grey iron shod door of the powder magazine loomed large, as if it were a gateway to another and better world. Fiddle reached into his back pocket and felt the smooth ridge of the tinderbox the captain had given him to mark his first year at sea; the day he'd earnt his promotion and reputation. By succumbing to the captain's passions, he'd become the foul joke; it was God's own truth, he'd paid the price for being Roger the Cabin Boy. He would end it all now.

The length of driftwood that had once been HMS Intrepid drifted lazily upon the warm Caribbean waters. Upon it sat one black cat, with a white tipped tail, and one ragged eared tabby cat; nose to nose, eyes wide, in the deep darkness of a cloud covered night.

'What happened?'

'I'm not exactly sure…'

'Looks like your tail was right after all, trouble was coming.'

'The tail knows.'

'Yes, the tail knows… oh well better get going, nice to see you again Giles, look after yourself, don't let the fleas get you down;' Fred Bastet 8ᵗʰ Heavenly Cat, lord overseer of spite, disappeared in a lightless flash.

'I don't have fleas… you have fleas.' Giles snarled into the darkness.

THE CATS OF PARIS

Let us begin here then, at the green front door, to the left of the Café de la Mouloud, in the Place Saint-Sulpice; where the coffee drinking thinkers are gathering to gossip. As you stand before the door, key in hand, you hear their laughter, their raised voices discussing jazz, phenomenal phenomenology, palindromes, poetry, politics, sex, and the delightful absurdity of existence. The thickening rue of cigarette smoke and sweat seeps through the café's door; you can smell their youth, the intoxicating joy of being young and dissatisfied. Poets and Paris, how they love to wage war on one another. As you turn the key, you see the scar within the plaster for the hundredth time; it's just another bullet wound, a glancing blow in a world still trying to come to terms with the madness of a just past, just war. The mark of a Nazi bullet that would have taken the head-off an anonymous stone thrower; if the pursuing German hadn't lied to his Oberfeldwebel about his deteriorating eyesight – a syphilitic consequence of indulging in too many unregistered Parisian streetwalkers; a case of life saved by lust? One day the bar's owner will agree to settle a bill in exchange for the wall's repair; and forever after, point to the unseeable mark and claim; 'The Nazi's tried to kill my bar but failed.'

The green door opens, you step inside the lobby, to greet an ossuary of umbrellas, abandoned walking sticks and forsaken canes. A tyreless bicycle wheel, stares from its nail on the wall, overlooking the stairway; but who could it belong to? None of the residents know, no one has ever known - yourself included - but there it stays, still staring at the stairs because, surely it would be unlucky to remove it now. A lifeless iris, ever watchful, watching over all; the flotsam of modern living, elevated to the position of a household god; how very 20th century. You give the god a nod, it's just what you do, and climb the stairs, heading up.

The first floor is deserted now, as 'Mme Guiliano's Secretarial School & Services,' opens at 9:00 and closes at 18:00 (with an hour and ten for lunch). Mme Guiliano's school teaches typing, shorthand, and archiving; and offers translation services for documents under five thousand words in four languages; English, German, Spanish and Italian. Mia is a straight-backed woman with sharp intelligent eyes, and a glare that would make a shitting dog whimper at forty paces. The infamous stare, and her ability to spot grammatical errors from across a room, have earned her the moniker 'Mia the Sniper.' She brokers no nonsense from her young students, undergoes paroxysms of rage when her Swiss made typewriters dare to malfunction, and won't have idle chit chat in working hours. Every girl that's ever been through her training school will tell you she's a hard taskmaster, and a gem. For she may be an exacting mistress but 'Mia the Sniper,' can also spot an empty stomach, a broken-heart, and an unwanted pregnancy from ten paces, and she will not see one of her young ladies inconvenienced, by society, tradition or men – which, in Mia's cold stone eyes, are all much the same thing. When the Germans occupied Paris, they attempted to commandeer the schools' services for the Third Reich; but Mia wasn't having it. Could there be anything more preposterously male than Nazism? She refused to comply to their demands, and spent three nights in the Montluc prison for her morals. Her girls say the Gestapo gave her back because they couldn't stand the glare; the truth is Mia agreed to watch over the comings and goings of Place Saint-Sulpice, and report on any suspicious activities she witnessed. And true to her word, Mia handed in weekly reports on the inhabitants and businesses of Saint-Sulpice until the end of the war; and a duller piece of fiction has never been created. Mia keeps a personal letter of thanks from General De Gaulle in her desktop drawer, nobody but her and the general have ever seen it. But now, as the wooden noticeboard on the landing says, the school is closed for the evening, so keep going, there's a way to go until you can unload the secret burden of your coat pocket.

The wall of the second-floor lobby bears a brass name plate, Dr A Merchin M.D and Dr B Merchin M.D. Not a couple as many visiting patients presume, but twin brothers born in the building, two floors above the one they now own, fifty-two years ago, just as the century was turning. Alain has the rooms to the left of the lobby, and Baptiste the rooms to the right. Each has their own consulting room, their own lounge, their own study, and bathrooms. But by way of adjoining dressing rooms, they share a bedroom and a bed, as they have since birth. In fifty-two years, they have never spent more than three nights apart. They were five years old when Alain was hospitalised due to a grumbling appendix; three nights of unparalleled, sleepless terror followed, which they swore to each other would never be repeated. Both are respected experts in their respective fields; but 'physician heal thyself,' they could not, nor each other. Each now falls asleep dreading they will wake to find the other dead. Neither has the courage to tell his brother his fears. You pass quickly and quietly over the parquet landing, in order not to disturb the slumbering brothers, a mark of respect for the doctors; whose sleeping habits are only known to you, because their cleaning woman, Madame Potins, loves to gossip. Potins cleans many of the flats, as well as Mme Guiliano's school and the Café below, so there isn't much about anybody that everybody doesn't know. But not even nosey Potins could guess what you get up to at night, or why the weight in your coat pocket puts a spring in your step; go on, up you go.

It was here, halfway between the second and third floor landing that M. Durant met his end twenty-years ago. A staunch Napoleonist, an avid phalerist, and defender of the nation's moral compass, Philipe Durant rushed from the family home to attend a lecture on fourteenth century heraldry, with a chunk of unbuttered baguette in his hand. He bit into the bread on the fourteenth step, only to have it lodge in his throat on the thirteenth; he stumbled down the twelfth, fell on the tenth and passed from this conscious plain on the ninth. He was found spreadeagled on the doctors' parquet landing later that evening by Daniel Roebuck; an American professor of architecture, renting a room —-your room now as it happens - on the fifth floor, during his six-month sabbatical in the capital. The Widow Durant, as she is now known, still lives in their old apartment, but it is now much reduced, being only the rooms on the right side of the stairs instead of the whole floor. Following her late husband's example, the Widow Durant, remains a staunch Napoleonist, but limits her political expression to sartorial elegance. She wears a sash of deep Napoleonic blue on the emperor's birthday, and her husband's service medal (he was a cartographer during the last six months of the Great War) on Bastille Day; and has her half of the landing carpeted in a hard wearing deep plum pile, that a canny salesman erroneously assured her was the same colour used in Napoleon III's private rooms. The rooms to the left of the stairs are occupied by M.

Perrin and family, with the exception of the largest room, nearest the landing, which is rented by C.D & Frères, a small but renowned firm specialising in protecting the intellectual properties of ceramic tile decorators. A hotly contested arena that has the firm's three employees out of the office three days out of every five. This leaves the running of the office in the capable hands of Marie Poulet, a thirty-five-year-old, failed trombonist from Nice, with a taste for chicory coffee and straight thigh confining skirts. Marie has worked for C.D & Frères for four years and is now so adept at her job, she can spend two thirds of her working day reading romance novels, or looking out of the office window, in order to scrutinise the young men that linger in the Place Saint-Sulpice. Conveniently for Marie, her assessments of the men beneath her window, always finds them beneath her contempt; which permits her lurid imagination to do whatever it might with them; whilst maintaining her cold distance and severe frosty virginity.

The three rooms behind C.D & Frères have been occupied by the Perrin family since the second year of the war. In that time, three children have been born; the eldest Jean, has a laugh like a donkey, and ricket warped legs; giving his determination to be a goalie for France, an air of tragedy he is not yet old enough to appreciate. His sister Charlotte, contracted tuberculosis at the age of five and is seldom out of bed. Home-schooled by Mme Perrin, who does her best, but will freely admit she has never read a book in her life, and can only do sums in multiples of two, is rightfully proud of her daughter. For despite these health and educational disadvantages, Charlotte can do long division, has read Voltaire and Proust (books given to her by Mme Guiliano, who has spotted the girl's potential), and can finish Le Figaro's crossword with very little help from other family members before bedtime. The youngest son, Claude is an utter bastard. He's a dark-eyed, mean, self-centred child, who enjoys nothing more than mocking his older brother's walk, his sister's incapacity and his mother's inability to tell the time. He is of course his father's favourite, and is destined for a position of authority in a local abattoir, which will go some way in protecting society from some of his more appalling desires. You rather like him too; birds of a feather and all that. The Perrin's carpet is threadbare and red, a striking contrast to Widow Durant's Napoleonic blue; the two carpets meet in the middle of the landing, the colours of revolution and heraldic tradition side by side, where the stairwell intersects the lobby. M. Perrin, a kindly man with a moustache Renoir would have revelled in, is devoted to his wife and children, and never regrets a moment, or looks back on lost opportunities. 'Non, je ne regrette rien,' is his moto and his song, as he works diligently day in day out; a minor accountant manager, in a minor bank. But sometimes, he sneaks naked from his apartment, lays his pale, pallid body along the intersecting carpets – and envisions himself as the living embodiment of the tricolore, a true son of France.

The fourth floor has been much altered over the years; some would say much abused. Like its lower brothers it was once two apartments but was soon split into three and then four. Flat 4a, to the far right of the building, is now occupied by Mlle Blanchard, the granddaughter of the building's original owner Henri Blanchard. Although unquestionably bourgeois, Sophie Blanchard feels she has been twice cursed, firstly she's been unable to secure her inheritance without selling or renting out portions of her estate to people she detests; and secondly, she inherited her grandfather's impressive height and sour looks. It was once said of her illustrious grandfather, that he had the bearing of an oak and the face of a crab-apple. The same could certainly be said of Sophie. As many tall women do, Sophie has spent much of her life trying to hide her height with a self-conscious stoop, but there was nothing she could do to hide her crab-apple face; outside of a hessian vail or a paper bag. Now in her eighties, her timid stoop has become a marked hunch, which in combination with her dreadful countenance, has earnt her the nickname 'the witch.' She was christened as such by that Perrin boy to be exact, or so Mme Pontis, that dreadful old gossip has told her. It's a slight Sophie has taken to heart, and now she rarely goes out. The resentment Sophie feels for fate's slings and arrows, is only matched by her resentment, for those she is forced to share her family home with – she'd kill them all if she could; she curses them all daily, as she bends over the bubbling pot of her seething stew.

On the other side of the landing, Flat 4b, the apartment nearest the stairs; is where you'll find Otto Banks, a trained cabinet maker and retired puzzle cutter from Vienna. Otto was once a close acquaintance and devotee of Wilhelm Reich; the Freudian Psychoanalyst, author of 'The Mass Psychology of Fascism' (1933), and discoverer or perpetrator (depending on your viewpoint) of the theory of Orgone energy. Otto will tell anyone who sits still long enough that Wilhelm came to him for guidance on the appropriate joints for his Orgone Accumulators; an invention Reich was sure would change the world. And this is perfectly true, but what is even truer is that Otto wanted a cut of the projected profits, and refused to participate in the venture when his offer was rebutted. This not only ended the men's friendship but in the dark decade that followed, left Otto with a niggling suspicion that the Orgone Accumulators might have worked, and war avoided. If only he'd been less self-centred and Wilhelm less greedy, countless lives would have been saved; and he'd live in a better apartment. Reich now visits Otto every night with blueprints for more ingenious, humanity saving, Orgone reaping devices; that he will not reveal until Otto signs away his rights, and every night Otto refuses, and so Wilhelm dissipates into the morning's Organosphere, and the world is a less orgasmic place for his passing. 'Not everything's about you,' Mme Pontins tells him, but alas Otto knows better.

The door to 4c is open, you look inside as you always do, and see a forest. An expanse of dappled shade vying with beams of verdant light, a scene of idyllic beauty that seems to go on forever. This is the home of Morris Bunn, an English army veteran, and his door is always open. Morris saw France for the first time from a landing craft, when approaching the beaches of Normandy. During his terrifying and violent journey across France, Morris and three of his buddies, Norm, Sid and Pete, became separated from their unit and took shelter in an abandoned farmhouse. In the farmhouse's cramped cellar, they discovered a surfeit of wine and pickled vegetables. Being hale and hearty lads, they set about demolishing the stash with gusto; just as a retreating artillery unit decided to demolish the farmhouse with die heftigkeit. Norm was blown to pieces; Sid never knew what hit him and Pete was killed when the farmhouse fell on top of his head. Morris was blown into the cellar, and that is where he was found a month later, sipping red wine and eating pickled onions, whilst talking to pieces of Norm. Morris was shipped back to Blighty and taken to a hospital where the staff spoke gently, and the patients were given plenty to do. But Morris could no longer stand to be locked in. At first, he insisted on being by a window, and then he insisted on being by an open door, and then he insisted on sleeping outside the door, and then in the hospital garden; and then the hospital insisted he left. Unable to hold down a job or have a door closed on him without disintegrating into a wailing ball of terror, Morris lived on the streets of London for three years, a vacant space in an aging demob suit. Until one morning whilst rummaging through a Hyde Park litterbin he discovered a discarded set of children's chalks. An hour later the pavement before him looked like a field of meadow flowers, and Morris couldn't say how it had happened. Somebody threw him sixpence, someone else threw in a farthing, then a shilling came calling and another and another; and within an hour he had a quid in his pocket. And he would have got more if the Old Bill hadn't turned up and felt his collar; 'Move on now or you're nicked.' Nicked meant a cell for the night; not what Morris needed, so he scarpered. It was then Morris made what he would later call the 'great decision.' He suddenly had options and options require a decision and as every decision may cancel other options; each decision had to be considered; 'do I buy fags, a pint or more chalks?' Morris bought a load of chalks, and a packet of Senior Service; it was a great decision. Two months later he'd been chased off every park and thoroughfare north of the river. He could feel the heat closing in on him with their devil dolls. They were calling him a vandal, a public menace, a 'bleedin' pain in the arse!' – but Morris felt like an artist, and where else should an artist go but Paris? After four years in his adopted capital, Morris' French is basic at best. But who needs to talk when you can conjure up a waterfall on a curb? Morris has embraced everything France has to offer. He's given up Senior Service for Gitanes, and although he'll never eat another pickled onion again for as long as he lives, he has learnt to appreciate red wine, and as far as he's concerned, a good mushroom omelette knocks pie and mash into a cocked hat. But he still can't be in a room if the door is closed, and as the Paris authorities don't let people sleep rough in their city, he had to bring the outside inside; and that's why Morris Bunn's room is filled with an endless vista of boundless space. Not a stick of furniture though; but you can't have everything, mustn't grumble ah! The English, what an odd lot they are – go on, you've had your look, move on.

The last flat on the fourth floor, 4d, on the far left of the building is the smallest flat of all, comprising of two small box rooms with a thin interconnecting corridor. In Henri Blanchard's day, the rooms were used to store winter coats and hat boxes, although they were also occasionally used by servants for erotic rendezvous. Obviously, Henri Blanchard was unaware of this but his wife, François Blanchard was very much aware of these shenanigans, but never said a word as she found watching the help go at it, very educational and invigorating. Which given her husband's crab-apple face was inspiration she sorely needed. The rooms are now occupied, haunted by the thin frame of M. Breut. A Parisian born and bred; Pierre Breut has lived with tuberculosis since the age of twelve. He is now twenty-four but looks fifty-eight and feels seventy. When Breut first realised he was not long for this world he determined to live each day as if it was his last, to fill his days with pleasure, beauty, and excellence. It just so happens that M. Breut finds pleasure, beauty, and excellence in the practice of philately. For him the gummed backed stamp is a mark of man's enterprise and culture. It signifies exotic destinations, mystery, travel and adventure, and all captured perfectly within the precise, tight, tiny frame of ordered bureaucracy, that is a stamp. M. Breut, is an uncommonly dull man, which is why nobody talks to him more than they have to; and being in the room he's in, nobody has to. So, moving on quickly, lest M Breut should appear, you climb up the staircase to the fifth floor, the servants' quarters, the garret flats. Four identical, perfectly proportioned single rooms for rent; shared occupancy an option. The rooms have no numbers, as there's no point, mail seldom comes and if it does, Mme Pontins would already have read it, and if it's an official document, a summons or a demand, you can count on the denizens of the fifth floor to make sure you never get it.

The rooms have three occupants at present, young Jules from Lille, a mad about jazz, jazz drummer who arrived three months ago with a snare drum and six sticks. He works long sweaty days downstairs in the café's kitchen and spends his nights sitting in on late night jazz sessions. He barely sees the sun from one week to the next, but Jules has never been happier. He thinks he can do this forever; but he's young, he'll learn. And if the four flights of stairs and Benzedrine don't kill him, he'll return to Lille one day with some great stories, and an STD that he'll pass onto his childhood sweetheart, so they'll both have something to remind them of Paris. And then there's Milo, dear old Milo, sixty-four going on seven. A child in an old man's body. Milo loves riding the Metro and has done so every day for the last fifty-two years. All the ticket collectors and guards know him and let him be: it's Milo, he's not hurting anybody. It's true he never has, not a soul, not an animal or insect could be found to say a bad word about dear old Milo. And yet every night, when Milo goes to bed at eight, he weeps for all the bad things he thinks he's done. He weeps for being fat, for being stupid, for being ugly, for being untidy, for breaking his Mama's heart, and for letting her die. At night Milo is inconsolable until he's asleep, and in the day he's miserable until he's on the Metro; and then all is right in the world of Milo. What will become of him? Poor dear Milo. You might have to take care of that one of these days, it would be a mercy really.

No carpet on this floor, not even polish on the bare boards. Step quietly now. Listen, is Milo crying? No, that's his snore; bless him. Jules will be downstairs or at some jazz bar, waiting his turn to beat the skins; good luck to him, good luck to all jazz crazed youth, long may they rave. But you, however, have had enough. It's been a long day. You've climbed the stairs; you're fit to drop. Each day has enough worries of its own; isn't that what the good Lord said? He should know, they crucified the bastard. True, but there's still a few things to do before you can write this day off. You open the door and step into the room, your room. Head down, shoulders hunched to avoid the low beam, you'll end up looking like that old witch on the third floor if you're not careful; no worries there, you've got plans, you're going places, but first things first. Kick your shoes off and breathe. The air is hot and stale and full of dust, but it's your dust, and you're not asking anybody else to share it, so sod it. You reach into your coat pocket and pull out a bloody bundle of discoloured serviettes. It's just a few chicken livers; nothing nasty going on here. You set the bundle on an old tin plate you keep under the palette you call a bed; then get the old knife you keep under the folded blanket you use as a pillow; it's just for show, you could ride bareback to

Marseille on that blade and not feel a thing. Now chop the liver up, nice and small. Now get that small blue bottle; and sprinkle liberally but mind your fingers we don't want any black tongues around here; nice job. Now that's done, carry the plate over to the corner of the room and look up – and there's the starry, starry night looking down on you through the cracked window that some might call a skylight. You push the latch to one side and force the window up; giving you just enough room to get out onto the roof.

And there you sit, with Paris at your feet and the Café de la Mouloud under your arse. You hold the plate high above your head and wait. And here they come, the cats of Paris, running over the slanted roofs to greet you; well greet your food, you've no allusions about that, cats are cats, nasty greedy little bastards. Sleek, thick, thin, moth eaten and in the prime of life they come, the nasty little brutes, pushing their stinking bodies against you, rubbing against your thighs, tails erect like walking pricks, straining to get at your plate of chicken livers – purring like drum rolls, but not for much longer.

And there at your feet is a little tabby cat with wide eyes and a ragged ear. Someone's taken a bite out of that bastard, what a scrawny little bugger, better he wasn't here at all. You reach up and flick a sliver of liver towards him; it lands at his feet. You watch and wait, holding your breath. The scrappy little bugger just sits down, winds his tail around his feet and looks at you. That blank soulless cat stare; that 'why are you still here?' stare. It makes your skin crawl… bloody cats. You really want to lash out, give him a kick and send him over the edge; what wouldn't you give to see that! But it would only startle the other cats; best to sit and wait and watch the show. The perfect way to end an evening, clear the roofs of vermin and get to bed with a clean conscience, in a job well done. You set the plate down and watch them rush in – the ragged eared tabby jumps in spitting, back raised, ears twitching – and all the other cats back off, sit down and start to preen. You're sitting in a circle of grooming, self-satisfied cats, and not one of them is eating the poisoned liver. The tabby with the ragged ear pushes against your shin, you kick out, miss, slip and slide - CAREFUL NOW – that could have been nasty, another metre or so and you would have gone over the side. You edge yourself back, pick up the plate and throw it at the tabby, hard enough to take his head off; but the cat dodges and the plate skips off the roof and down into the street. What a waste of good strychnine; what a perfectly awful way to end a day. The tabby is at it again, pushing against your thigh now. You reach out to grab it and throw it over, but it lashes out and strikes your finger with its claws. You jump to your feet, kicking at the brute, calling down all the curses you can muster; and your finger hurts! Ouch, suck the wound clean and… that taste, that's not liver. Bugger!

The suicide that threw himself into the Place Saint-Sulpice, was recorded in the next day's evening paper. Not because of the manner and clear determination he had to end his life; self-poisoning and jumping from a high building were not unheard-of strategies; but because the desperate act of a lonely individual – name as yet unknown – also ended the life of Mme Pontins, a well-known local character, as she was leaving her place of work. It was a tragedy, and a tragedy that could have been so easily avoided, as the paper asserted, 'if people reached out to one another, enquired about their neighbours, and took more than a passing interest in one another's lives, surely such tragedies would become a thing of the past. Paris is the city of light and enlightenment, we are a city of a million individuals, and we need to reach out to one another, share our light and talk,' … and as anyone who knew Mrs Pontins could testify, she'd want people to talk.

KITAMORPHOSIS

Giles Bastet awoke after a night of disturbing dreams to find himself transformed into a female human. His lovely stripey fur had been replaced by a hideous baldness; just looking at the soft rounded lines turned his stomach. How had this happened? Had he done this terrible thing to himself? No, that wasn't possible, so the question was, who had done this terrible thing to him? So, who had the power? Only Mother? If so, somebody must have been telling lies about Giles, because he could see no reason for Holy Mother Bastet (Blessed be her name) to do such a thing, and anyway she wasn't the type to be so vindictive, not on a whim, not without a warning. No, it couldn't be Mother, so who could have done such a spiteful... of course, it had to be Fred; Fred Bastet 8th Heavenly Cat, lord high overseer of spite.

Giles ran through the command that would summon his brother; a twitch of the tail, a crossing of a whisker, and a ripple of the fur... but his talking tail was gone, as were his whiskers and his fur. He'd been stripped of his powers, rendered human and mortal... he really wasn't sure which was worse. He had to admit, Fred had really out done himself this time.

But where was Fred? Why wasn't he here gloating over his victory? It wasn't like Fred to miss such an opportunity. And where was here? A small empty room, bare except for the shelves that lined three of the walls; all of which were empty; and not a clue how he got there. Giles padded around in a circle to steady his nerves, but it felt wrong and hurt his knees. He tried to wash himself but the feel of his smooth tongue on his smooth skin made his stomach churn; and his back wouldn't bend as it should, so he couldn't have washed his butt if he wanted to. His feet were horrific, the ugliest things he'd ever seen, so graceless, flat, and inflexible. Pushing his toes into the floor Giles tried to stand, but his ungainly long legs buckled beneath him, and he fell flat on his face. How did the humans do it? Giles' nose ached; how did they walk around with these things so high up on their bodies? They must have constant backache, and what if you dropped something? How could you pick it up? How was one supposed to balance on two legs without a tail? As far as he could see the entire human body was useless, even Giles' ragged ear was better than the lifeless stumps he had stuck to the sides of this bulbous blob of a head. He looked to his front paws and saw fingers. He'd always admired the servant's fingers. Fingers that can fiddle, make, and create, fingers to scratch and preen; but what was the point if he didn't have any fur?

Although the room was empty, there was an odour, a sour, rich aroma he couldn't place with his new and utterly useless throbbing snout. But there was something about the smell that reminded him of Egypt, and that Greek Egyptian queen, what was her name? Bumps rose along the bare skin of the female arm; the skin on the legs quickly followed suit; what did it mean? His nipples - only two, what was the point of that? - were suddenly hard and uncomfortable. The body executed an involuntary flutter that Giles recognised; the body was cold, he was cold, the room was cold, and getting colder. He had to get out of the room or freeze. Giles shuffled his new ungainly body towards the door and rubbed his clawless fingers against it; but nobody came. He tried to miaow but all he did was let out a most unsatisfactory breathy whine. Using both hands Giles took hold of the doorknob and pulled – the door resisted. He tried pulling downwards – nothing happened. How did the servants do this? Was he stuck in this room forever? If he couldn't get out, how did he get in? How did he end up in this room? Giles sat back on what should have been his haunches – which felt entirely wrong – and tried to picture the last place he remembered himself actually being himself. There'd been the model village, the park, that tower block with the talkative kitty, and of course Basingstoke, bloody Basingstoke... but where was the last place he'd been? Of course, the dairy. At first he'd just wanted to see goats – why he couldn't say – their eyes perhaps, so silly, all in the wrong way round, so amusing; and then he'd heard the cows. He watched as they filed compliantly into the milking shed, all big and lumbering; not a thought in their huge heads, heavy with milk, covered in shit. Was it any wonder the servants preferred dealing with these docile beasts to the mischievous comedian goats? And then of course, there was the milk. Its all about the product with those humans; they didn't just want enough milk; they wanted a surfeit with more to spare. Giles had watched the mechanised milking with some interest; you had to give it to these humans; the prime mammalian activity handed over to machines; truly amazing. Giles had often wondered about the human's fascination with machines. Perhaps deep down they actually wanted to be machines? Perhaps that's why they lived the kind of lives they did, because they yearned to be unthinking, unfeeling devises free from the concerns for the slings and arrows of outrageous misfortune. Giles had to admit it would be easier than trying to live in a body without fur or whiskers; if this is what it felt like to be human, why not become a machine? It might improve their service.

Giles recalled following the tubes and pipes from the milking shed to a sealed metal tower which must have contained enough milk to float a boat; did the humans drink it or bathe in it – like that Greek Egyptian queen did, yes that was it, she smelt of milk, but what was her name?

Another set of pipes connected the milk towers to a large boxy looking building; Giles just had to know what was going on in such a dull looking place; what were they doing with all that milk? A swish of the tail and a stretch of a claw projected him beyond the wall and into a labyrinth of shiny metal pipes and whirring steel machines.

In and out of the labyrinth scuttled a multitude of industrious humans in white coats, blue aprons, and blue hairnets. Giles rather liked the look; it reminded him of the painted heads of the Egyptian priests; what was their queen's name? Giles felt a sharp spasm shoot through his poorly packed guts; was it any wonder humans were so miserable; eating must be a torture for them. Focus, focus, what happened next… the pipes, the shiny machines and the humans running around like rats in a maze. What were they making?

Cleopatra, that was it. The Greek Egyptian queen was called Cleopatra, and she didn't smell of milk; no, it was cheese. They were making cheese. He'd seen milk churns before but never on this scale. Now the humans had machines to do the actual hard labour, but he recognised the process. He watched as four humans gathered around a long metal trough filled with thickening milk, and began stirring it with long hollow metal oars, as the curds and whey separated; oh yes he recognised the process alright, only humans could turn lovely flowing milk into bricks of stinky cheese. A metaphor perhaps? There was something about the randomness of life that scared humans; yes life's arbitrary nature scared them silly. They just couldn't go with the flow, and see what happened, everything had to be solid and certain. Which is why they wanted to be machines and live predictable lives. It was obvious really; Giles wondered why he'd never thought of it before? Was it really any wonder humans were at their happiest when in service to a higher power? Giles' naked skin shivered. He felt a hot fist at the centre of his stomach tighten as he thought; 'is this all my fault?' Had he driven mankind to build this modern world of stupefying order because of their fear of him? Man served his gods, gods like his Holy Mother Bastet, to be safe from misfortune; but he and his brothers and sisters were that misfortune. Humans wanted to be machines because of him. Man was mechanising the world, to be safe, to protect themselves from the will of the gods… but what would become of him? Giles Bastet, 9_{th} heavenly cat, lord high overseer of malfunction… that sounded dreadful. As did the word overseer, what was an overseer at the end of the day? Not a creator, with agency and power, but a watcher, a secondary service dependent on those who acted… if he followed that line of thinking; then he was dependent on humans; he was in service to them! What was this introspection? What was this self-doubt? Was this what it was to be human and in need of a god?

They'd seen him; 'There's a cat in here!' 'How did it get in?' 'Stop production!' 'It's a bloody moggy!' 'Cover the cheese!' 'The batch will be ruined!' 'GET IT OUT!'

They really shouldn't have tried to chase him. He would have left if they'd asked him to; probably. But going after him with their brooms, cheese harps and metal oars, was a mistake; what did they think was going to happen? He was the overseer of accidental death for crying out loud.

Images folded in on one another as they sped through Giles' human head; a swung broom clattered against a cheese harp and fell to the floor, tripping a man, who shoved his pal forward into the mesh of pipes, these snapped beneath his weight, sending a spout of milk arcing across the floor and into the eyes of the guy with the metal oar, who fell backwards crushing his coccyx against the milling machine's conveyer, that dragged his arm into the teeth of the mill which sent the metal oar spinning into the jaw of the man who fell to his knees in agony, causing his buddy to tumble over his back and land head first in the mechanised cheese cutter that severed his head, which projected a jet of blood into the gathering pool of milk, that washed around the feet of the next wave of shouting humans, that chased Giles up onto the humming metal box, the charging hoard slid on the milk, collided with the humming metal box, prompting Giles to take to the rafters and severing the power cable that electrified the pool of bloody milk; in which the thrashing hoard now lay; killing all but one… a young woman with braided blonde hair beneath her blue net beret. She looked up at Giles, high above the misery and mess and then at her fallen comrades and screamed and screamed until the walls of the factory reverberated with her cries. Giles remembered an old adage about spilt milk and would have shared it with the woman, if only she'd stop screaming for a moment; but she didn't, and then his ears began to hurt. Her scream echoed in his whiskers. He could feel it aching his fur, pulling at the roots of his claws; she had to be stopped. Giles saw her tonsils oscillating – and jumped in.

Giles felt the body vibrate. His stomach churned and tightened. He recognised the feeling – he was going to be sick – he gagged, retched and threw-up the mother of all furballs. He was free. Giles shook his fur clean and sniffed at the undulating pile of ooze at his feet; and saw within it, a white coat, a blue apron, a blue hairnet, a lung or two; and far, far, far too much cheese. He watched as what might once have been a head sank to the floor without volition, a last breath rising from its nostrils, faintly steaming. As a god, it wasn't often he had a new experience, and even rarer an experience he didn't care to repeat; but this certainly had been one. Cheese before bedtime; a recipe for disaster, to be so sick, like a dog.

MODERN SLAVERY SCANDAL BLAZE

The centre of town was brought to a standstill on Monday morning, when two fire engines attended a blaze at 17 Market Square.

The ensuing gridlock sealed off the town for four hours. The investigation that is to follow is likely to scar our town for years to come.

The charred remains of Richard Stinchcombe, a well-known local philanthropist, and founder member of the Benchley School of Dance, was recovered from the building at six o'clock that evening. His reputation like 17 Market Place, his family home, and renowned dance studio, has been razed to the ground.

Three as yet unidentified females had been rescued by the brave members of Benchley's Volunteer Fire Service within minutes of the alarm being raised. However, due to the intensity of the blaze, the proximity of other buildings and the danger the fire would spread to our historic town hall, the services of the Bennington engine were called on to assist in controlling the fire. Quite by chance Viktor Bulgakov, a Polish national, and most recent member of the Benington Volunteer Fire Service was on duty that morning. On arriving at the scene, Mr Bulgakov reports seeing one of the recently rescued women struggling with the paramedics that were trying to take her to hospital. 'I recognised the language as Latvian. And so went to see if I could be of assistance. It was then that I recognised the word the woman was repeating – дети – children, little ones. There were children still in the building's basement.' Thanks to Bulgakov's rapid actions, a team of firefighters was dispatched to the basement of an adjoining building, which was breached, and access to 17 Market Place gained. Attending Senior Fire Officer William Burrows, reports that twelve children were found within the basement, some of whom were manacled to the wall. It took three fire officers, ten minutes to free the children. Minutes later the entire building collapsed.

Although an official investigation has yet to commence, it seems that Mr Stinchcombe was part of a wider 'human trafficking' operation with connections in Eastern Europe. This paper is able to reveal that Stinchcombe was arrested five years ago in Manchester as part of the 'county lines,' investigation, but was soon released with no charges, as there was insufficient evidence to secure a conviction. It is believed that the local constabulary were unaware of his arrest, possibly due to the Manchester warrant and subsequent investigation, being carried out under his original name of Stirchley. However, unnamed sources have claimed that Stinchcombe's generous donations to local charities, which included the Police Benevolent Fund may have blinded local officials to his true nature.

All three women and twelve children are being assisted by the authorities. Under new government rules the minors will be able to apply for asylum but those that wish to return home will be assisted in doing so. Mr Denner M.P for the Benchley district, said; 'the treatment these individuals have received in our land is abhorrent. An insult to our humanity and theirs. Criminal gangs prey on the poverty and dreams of the desperate, whilst depending on the collusion and complicity of other's prejudices, to keep their foul work silent. Modern slavery is like old slavery, it only survives because people think you can be silent and still innocent. You cannot. We must all be vigilant and speak out against such barbarity wherever we find it.' When asked why he'd voted against the Modern Slavery Act in 2015, Mr Denner replied he didn't vote against it but abstained on purely procedural grounds.

Reports from the local hospital where three of the children are being treated for smoke inhalation and malnutrition, are described as positive. Medical Director Dr Benway, say the children are doing well, and should be released by the end of the week.

Mr Stinchcombe was not the only casualty of the fire. Despite the best efforts of the brave men and women of the Volunteer Fire service; the captive children's beloved pet cat is believed to have been lost in the fire. Unknown to Stinchcombe, the children had kept the cat for several weeks, but upon its discovery on Monday morning,

Stinchcombe tried to remove the cat from the house, moments before the blaze started. The cause of the blaze has yet to be identified.

Editor's Note: We ask should any readers spot a small tabby cat with a ragged right ear in the vicinity, to inform the office directly as the children are longing to be reunited with their treasured playmate.

CATACOMBS

Angela Brickles, known as Angie, but never Ange, emerged from her tent, and tested the edge of her trowel with her thumb. She checked the hang of her toolbelt, and then the hang of her sports bra. Yesterday's surprise wardrobe malfunction - with guest appearance by 'the girls' - had been so humiliating it had taken all her courage not to jump on the bus and leave the dig for good. Getting up early before anybody else was the only way she could possibly walk back onto the site. That way, she would be there before anybody else woke up, and when the other students arrived, they'd find her hard at it, trowel in hand. Angie bounced on her heels, judged the compressed strangulating hold of the bra. There would be no encore, the girls were staying home today.

Checking the geophysics grid references on her iPad with the grid references on the daily dig worksheet, Angie set out into the cat's cradle of string lines, test pits and geo-tags that covered the site. According to Professor Houghton, somewhere under the string grids, topsoil and piles of flint were the last undiscovered vestiges of Calleva Atrebatum, the Roman origins of Silchester; and he should know he'd been working on the site for the last twenty years. Excavation of the town started in the nineteenth century and carried on sporadically throughout the twentieth, until it finally came under the remit of Reading University who maintained the site for fieldwork as part of their popular archaeological course. Three years ago, the site had been declared 'academically exhausted,' and closed. But now a previously wooded area was being cleared for an extension to the ever-sluggish A33; and so, the site was opened for a 'last chance' four week dig. Angie had given up a trip to Croatia to be there; the chance to unearth Calleva's secrets was too good an opportunity to miss. And she'd had a great time, it really was a dream come true, until her tits decided to pop out and say hello on the third day of the dig; right in Dr Houghton's face too; mortifying, absolutely mortifying.

The poet Henry Treece, in his ripping historical yarns for children (always the same story but a different setting), had suggested that Calleva was in fact the origins of Camelot, and Angie, despite knowing her history, had never been able to entirely shake-off the idea. Unlike many large Roman conurbations, Calleva Atrebatum remained occupied long after the Romans left Britain. One of the most continuously occupied sites in the British Isles; was now just a sleepy village in the commuter greenbelt, a windbreak between two enormous urban conurbations. Poor old Camelot, how the mighty had fallen into disrepair. But every archaeologist has the same dream; 'what if I make the find that changes the history books?' What if she, Angela Brickles could prove Silchester was Camelot? Silly, silly, daydreams, but such dreams helped her get top grades and kept her trowel sharp.

As Angie passed between two clearly defined grids; one running to the top of a slight incline and one running the length of the adjoining depression; she spotted a sleeping cat, curled up on the topsoil spoil at the end of the path. The last thing she or her colleagues needed was to be digging through a cat's litter tray first thing in the morning; it was best for kitty if kitty didn't hang around; rumour had it Professor Houghton kept an air pistol for just such events.

'Come on kitty, off you go now.' The kitty yawned, stretched, and then gave Angie a supercilious stare, checking her out from top to toe as it did so. 'Oh, checking out the merchandise are we?' Angie snorted, 'a boy kitty for sure? Typical male behaviour. Go on now, before the boss man gets here and puts a pellet in your arse.' The cat, a ginger haired tom with white cuffed paws, turned his back on Angie and strolled away, tail swinging. As Angie watched him go, she spotted another cat, a sleek white thing, slinking its way through the string of the upper grid, moving towards her. 'You too whitey, get yourself gone.' The cat sped past her, hot on the tail of the ginger tom. 'Bye, bye whitey. I just know I'm gonna be digging through cat shit this morning…' To her left she spied a milk chocolate brown cat with jagged, dark chocolate stripes rubbing itself against a metal post Geophysics had driven into the ground. 'What is this? A pussycat party. Go on you…' Another cat, a fat tabby, with dark circular rims around its eyes padded towards her, tail aloft, chin high. 'Where you off to Harry Potter? What is this place, pussycat junction?' Something rubbed against her leg; she looked down to see a calico kitty twisting itself around her feet. And then she saw it; a thin dark discolouration in the earth. It was no more than two centimetres in length but Angie recognised the mark of cast-iron. She levelled her iPad; took a shot, and dropped to her knees. The calico cat pushed its way into her side, 'Go away Kitty, not now.' The cat persisted, pushing so hard it nearly toppled her over; 'Oh give over kitty.' Angie felt the solidity of the metal, it was no mere scrap, it was part of something larger; a find? The cat stepped forward, sniffed at Angie's mud besmirched fingers, and sunk its teeth deep into her forefinger. 'You little shit!' Angie spat, swiping at the creature. The cat skedaddled; leaving Angie sucking the wound, 'That hurt pussycat. You vicious little prick. That was totally uncalled for!' Angie took her trowel, and hurriedly cleared away the topsoil from within a two-centimetre circle, revealing a cast-iron ring threaded through a carved stone dimple. Time for another photo; it was important to record everything correctly. What kind of stone was that? Even beneath its veil of dirt it had an odd luminescence. Rotating her toolbelt across her hip, Angie produced a round ended paint brush. Gently skimming it across the surface of the exposed stone, revealed a moon-white sheen, marbled with grey; was it marble then? Angie licked her still throbbing finger, rubbed it across the surface of the stone, mingling the remaining dust with spit and blood. It was smooth, cool to the touch. It had to be marble. Expertly worked marble. Angie sat back on her denim arse, and tried to check her pounding heart.

The door to Professor Houghton's shed was still closed, and no-one had yet emerged from the tents on the other side of the dig; what were they playing at? They should at least be stirring by now? Angie checked the time on her iPad; it was eight o'clock, where was everybody? Professor Houghton should certainly be in by now? Giving her iPad a second look, Angie checked the time, date and… idiot. It was Sunday. Of course it was bloody Sunday. You bloody stupid mare… but then again, more time to get the job done. Angie bounced onto her knees and got busy with the trowel. Approximately twelve centimetres out from the centre of the stone dimple, Angie found a straight edge. Following the edge in a northerly direction, she found a corner, and then worked backwards until she located the adjoining corner. Working across, under the dimple, she traced the edge through the topsoil; back up and along, and down again until she reached her starting point. And there it was, a marbled white stone; approximately twenty-four centimetres wide and sixty centimetres high – practically A4 sized; with a four-centimetre, cast-iron ring at its centre. But it wasn't a stone, nor was it a slab of squared-off marble. It not only had depth but also a lip, a thin earth filled rim running around the circumference of what must be a lid. She had found a box. A carved stone box; but didn't that make it a casket? A sarcophagus even? Angie sucked on her finger and told herself to: 'Calm the fuck down. It's just a marble stone box. In the middle of a field that used to be a Roman settlement.' Still no sign of life from the tents, were those lazy bastards ever going to get up? After taking another photo, Angie placed the iPad on a mound of earth; set the camera to Video and pressed; 'Record'.

Angie ran her thumbnail around the dark rim of the box, dislodging the age-old dirt. Not wanting to put any strain on the fragile iron ring she took hold of the upper adjoining corners, held her breath, and gently lifted the lid towards her knees, and then gently placed it face down on the path beside her; and exhaled. Her hands were shaking; 'Come on girl, get a grip.' Angie took a breath and held the iPad above the open box.

'It's a statue. It looks like stone, possibly marble, I'm not as up on my geology as I should be. But it's different, darker to the marble of the box, casket, that I discovered it in.' she liked the sound of that "I discovered." 'It could be soapstone but I'm guessing. I really do need to check up on my geology. The statue, in form, is a cat. A cat sitting in a classic feline pose…' The word "classic" rang like a bell in her head. Angie turned off the iPad and tossed it away. The statue looked ancient, in fact Ancient Egyptian. And what was a statue of an Ancient Egyptian cat deity doing in the south of England? Angie did a quick cross reference in her mind. The Cult of Bastet had been recorded in the Mediterranean during the Middle Kingdom, around the twelfth dynasty; way too early for a Celtic cross over. But the Romans could certainly have brought it over during or even after the fall of the Ptolemaic Dynasty, the Greek Egyptian rulers that came to an end with Cleopatra VII. It was possible, but not very likely. Had one ever been found this far North in Europe? It really shouldn't be there? It was wrong, it didn't belong. Angie wondered if it could be one of Professor Houghton's little pranks? He did like to test his students. It wasn't beyond him to bury a fake artefact to test them; but would he be so reckless with something so exquisite? This wasn't a fake…it was real, wasn't it? It looked genuine. She needed to touch it. Her 'straight A student' brain told her not to; but she needed to know. And if it was, she'd be the first, the first in two thousand plus years to touch it. Angie reached in, fingers trembling, felt the coolness of the stone against her throbbing forefinger, closed her hand around the sleek form, and lifted it clear of the box. She held it up to her cheek. It was as smooth as glass. This could be no fake. It was made of a beautiful dark, mottled stone that perfectly emulated the flecks of a tabby cat's coat; the word 'alabaster' floated into her head. Alabaster, soft and easy to carve but brittle too. Angie felt a jagged edge, and inspected the thing anew; there was a piece missing from the right ear, it looked like a jagged bite. Was that there before? Panic gripped her, had she damaged it? Angie checked the ground all about her and then checked the box, but there was nothing to find.

'Poor kitty, did you lose your ear before you went to bed?' Angie brought the thing to her lips and kissed its nose.

The world flashed red, and then went black.

Angie awoke to find the alabaster sculpture still clasped in her hand, held tight against her chest. She was laying on her back, looking up into a void that undulated with a thin weak light. Thin plumes of smoke rose from the wicks of bowl-shaped oil lamps set on either side of her. She coughed; the room echoed to the sound. Reaching into her toolbelt Angie produced her mobile phone; the screen's glow was a welcome sight, but there was no signal. Angie flicked through to the torch setting and reached out into the darkness with the thin beam. Her heart nearly jumped from her chest. She was laying at the centre of a gold lined room at the foot of a huge stone statue of the cat Goddess Bastet.

How did this happen? Had the ground collapsed beneath her? Had she fallen into some ancient temple? If so, it was one hell of a discovery; but if that was the case… where was the sky? Her 'straight A student' mind knew that couldn't be so. The Roman's didn't worship Bastet, and there was no way a secret cult could have built such a temple in the middle of a town and not been discovered… and besides, who lit the oil lamps? Panic rose like a tide of hot lava from the pit of her stomach; 'Who's there? What's going on?'

A black cat with a white-tipped tail stepped into her beam of light as it washed over the base of the statue. 'Hello kitty cat, want to show me the way out?' Before she'd finished the sentence another cat joined the other at the base of the statue, a tortoiseshell with shining green eyes, 'well ain't you pretty, come on now, why don't you show me how you got in here…' Two identical, blotchy black and white cats joined the others, a calico cat followed, hopping in from the darkness. 'Hay you look familiar, you remember me?' Angie heard the nervous edge in her voice as she felt the sharp tingle in her forefinger awaken. And then there were three more, a fat tabby cat, a sleek white cat and a ginger striped cat with piercing eyes; eight cats, all looking down on her, with hungry expectant eyes. Angie felt her throat tighten; 'Where did you all come from… I need to get out of here, come on kitty cats, show me how you got in here.'

The cats seemed to look at one another and then settled down to wait.

'Has anybody seen Giles?' The voice came from the base of the statue and echoed around the room, 'just like him to be late,'

'Who's there! Hello, hello. Can you hear me. Where am I? who's there? Can you hear me?' Angie could hear the panic in her own voice, and felt a scream rising from her centre, 'please, who is it? I'm scared. Who's there?'

A blue flash erupted to her left, 'Did somebody call me?'

'Giles, welcome. Late again, always the last.'

'Which is why we keep the best, until last.'

'Yes, very drole, now then, it seems this human has stumbled upon…'

It was the cats; the cats were speaking. Angie jumped to her feet, screamed, and ran into the darkness – straight into a huge brass gong

– the resulting clamour filled the darkness with an echo that could have split stone; and did. Angie looked up just in time to see the great stone head of Mother Bastet falling towards her. Their heads met. Angie's body slumped into the sand at the base of the statue.

'Well, that's just rude.'

'Nice one Giles.'

'It wasn't me.'

'I wonder what Mother will say about the damage you did to her statue....'

'It wasn't me Frank. In fact I'd say it was more an act of spite!'

'That's enough you two. The statue was damaged centuries ago. There was nothing but cobwebs holding its head in place. The question is, what are we going to do with her?'

'We could eat it.'

'No, I'd rather we didn't... anybody else want to eat the dead girl? No, in that case, I suggest we let time deal with it. I can't see us coming back here anytime soon, agreed? Right then... meeting adjourned. Nice seeing...'

The temple was illuminated by a series of blue flashes, and then fell silent. Giles stepped up to the fallen body and examined the remains. He had no idea who she was; he saw the alabaster statue laying by her side, what was that doing there, he hadn't seen that since... now where had that been?

There had been a little town not far from the coast. Lots of building work going on, damaged temples and damaged streets. That was it, there'd been an earthquake a short while before his arrival, and the townspeople were busy getting the place back together. It was an average Roman town, with all the standard Hellenistic temples, Apollo and the like, and a small Vespasian cult, and of course a bunch of ancestor worshippers. But Giles had come to see the temple that had been dedicated to his Grandmother Isis. He'd always been rather fond of his grandmother, despite some of her more wayward aspects. For a start it didn't seem to bother her that the humans depicted her as a female human with wings; an insult if there ever was one. And she did seem to enjoy a rather chaotic personal life, and some of her base drives were downright sordid; resurrecting the dead because you wanted to have sex with them was certainly a questionable practice. But she did seem to really care about the ordinary humans, especially the woman; and it just so happened at that time in his life, Giles had grown weary of the consequences of his being. As soon as he got to know a human, something dreadful happened to them. He was beginning to feel as if he was more of a curse than a god; and if there was anybody that could advise him on the matter it was Granma Isis.

The temple itself wasn't the grandest he'd ever seen, but it wasn't bad for a small town. It had snow white cotton drapes before the inner sanctum, and red drapes hanging from the walls inside it; and the statue to his grandmother wasn't bad, at least it didn't have those bloody awful wings. And it was good to see they had a statue to his mother in her rightful place, at the right hand of the Goddess Isis. She looked great, she always did. Giles' estimation of the place jumped several notches when he spotted nine smaller cat statues placed around the edge of the priest's altar. A nice touch indeed. Of course, the statue dedicated to him was the smallest, but at least his ear was complete. It was pleasing to see the proper respect being shown to his divinity. Giles sat down at the base of the statue, intoned the required greeting, and had just begun laying out his concerns to his grandmother's image when three priests, in long white robes, entered the inner sanctum swinging three large incense burners. They bowed to his grandmother and began circling the altar before her statue. Not seeing why their presence should interrupt his conversation, Giles turned his back on them and continued to lay out his concerns. And this is why, he couldn't be exactly sure what happened next – there was the sound of ripping material, a curse, a clatter and a commotion of raised voices, another curse and then a series of high-pitched wails. When Giles turned around, all three priests were lying in a flaming pile at the far corner of the altar, and three seconds later, they were running around screaming, their robes in flames.

'You see grandmother, this is what I'm talking about, it's becoming a real furball in the throat.'

One of the priests ran straight into the temple wall, knocking himself senseless, and igniting the red drapes. Another ran from the sanctum screaming, only to get caught up in the entrance's white drapes and tumble down the steps. The third priest, tore off his robes, picked up a burning censer and threw it out the sanctum's door; where it rolled down the steps, reigniting his drape wrapped colleague. He then tried to pick up another censer, but clipped the side of the altar, spilling the censer's entire contents across the floor, igniting the drapes on the other side of the wall. Giles leapt onto the altar, looked down at its base, and saw the damage done to his statue by the priest's clumsiness.

'You idiot! You've chipped my ear!'

The priest screamed and ran towards the Goddess Isis for protection. He launched himself into the statue's breast, flung his arms around her neck, and pleaded for mercy. The statue wobbled, spun and crashed to the floor.

'Oh, you've done it now fool, I'm going to make you sorry you were...' Giles felt a tremor run through the temple's foundations, followed by cries in the courtyard. He turned his tail on the fallen priest and strolled through the flames to investigate. 'Well, that makes sense...' A billow of smoke resembling a pine tree was streaming from the mountain behind the town. It was streaked with flashes of lightning and streaks of flames. Giles checked himself; is this me? It didn't seem likely, not his style. 'Grandmother? Is this you?' And then it began to rain ash and pumice stones the size of his head. 'Right then, I'm out of here.' And in a blue flash he was.

It was ten o'clock when the iPad was found by the shallow hole in the path to the spoil dump. The girl that found it took it to Professor Houghton in his shed, who checked the device's number against the stock sheet. They sent two girls to check Angela's tent, but she was gone. Most of her stuff was there but her tool belt and boots were missing. They tried the iPad to see if Angie had left a message, but it seemed - much against instructions – Angie had changed the passcode, so there was no way of knowing. They waited till lunchtime before trying to call her mobile, and when they did, they got no answer. By two o'clock they were considering calling the police. But Professor Houghton knew best, and he was certain that the young woman whose breasts had inadvertently fallen into his face, had done a runner. It looked as if his 'grade A student' was a thief. His prized artefact was missing too. He'd buried it on every Silchester dig to test the students; it was just a prank, but the looks on their young faces when they found it was priceless. Even more so when he told them it was actually from Pompei, a not altogether official gift for his work on the site in the seventies. And now it was gone. He'd have to write to her and ask her to return it. He really didn't want to involve the police, not if he didn't have to. Professor Houghton loaded his air pistol; somebody had reported cats on the site.

THE CAT'S THE ONLY CAT

Billy slumped down in the chair and put his feet up on the windowsill. Out there beyond his patent leather shoes New York glowed like a swarm of fireflies, but he didn't want anything to do with it. New York could stay out there or go to hell for all he cared. Everything he needed was in this hotel room, and he didn't need a lot. Truth of it was, he was needing less and less these days, less and less of that, but much more of the other. Billy shut his eyes and listened to the traffic; the noise of life. Sadly, the sounds of the city held no melody for him. It was discordant like some pre-war German cabaret; no it wasn't for him. He liked his music tuned and smooth, with plenty of swing. Billy turned his heavy head and saw the light dancing across the sax laying on the unmade bed; why was it out of its case? He hadn't played it in days; or had he? Billy licked his lips and felt the echo of the embouchure. So, he had been playing, a good blow by the feel of it too; when did that happen and where... no it was gone, like the tunes, like all good jazz; there for one night only and gone. It was a beautiful thing, the sax, a beautiful thing; with the light dancing across it - his saxophone, on his unmade hotel bed; a beautiful thing. He could watch it for hours; probably had. But nonetheless, if he had the energy; he'd throw the lot out the window; saxophone, bed and himself. Billy wanted there to be less. He wanted there to be nothing. But energy was one of the things Billy definitely had less and less of these days, so he did nothing. Billy had lost his swing, and all the fight had gone out of him, dissipated into the sweet numbness of the cure, yeah, that's right Billy had found his medicine.

There was a time, when he was young, when he'd been heavy with hate, soaked to the skin with it. He'd raged in a haze of hate, a walking fist of unfocused, unfathomable hate. But not anymore; those days, those dark days were gone. It just so happened that all the other days were going too. And he really didn't mind; he was a fading refrain in a lapsing lullaby; and that was just fine. There was no-one to stop him and no-one he cared to stop for, he wasn't hurting anybody but himself, and he wasn't hurting at all, no sir, the medicine made sure of that. Soon the song would end; he imagined a sustained sigh weaving between a natural minor scale and then melting into silence. That would be cool, a cool way to end a sad song. And there was nobody to blame but himself; and he wasn't in the blame game – he wasn't playing at all.

Billy used to tell himself he hated people, but it wasn't true. People were just there when he raged. They were just doors to batter against, doors to access the anger, and he was sick of battering against doors, they'd been too many doors in his life. Now he wanted to stay here, here in his hotel room with his saxophone and his unmade bed; to stay until he left, and he could feel himself leaving, feel the wave coming in.

It had taken him a long time to work out the truth about himself. Maybe because, deep down, instinctively he knew, when he heard the truth, it would be predictable; disappointing; like a jukebox song with no real art, no swing, no improvisation; just another cover version of a lame song. The truth will set you free, that's what the bible says; and if that's not proof of pure hokum, what is? The truth was this, life was too much. Too ugly, too beautiful, too intense, too weak, too loud, too bright, and so unkind; and it all disappointed Billy. The melody sucked and he couldn't play along with it. His range was limited; that was the truth of it. It was no excuse, certainly no reason; but it was the truth … the fault was within him. The rage he called anger wasn't anger at all, it was fear. He wasn't angry, he was terrified.

Billy had been scared for so long he ached. His shoulders ached with the weight of carrying his fear. His legs ached with the need to flee he kept bound-up within them; and his teeth, oh his poor, poor teeth, they were shattering with the pressure of three tonnes of terror per square inch he placed on them every time he smiled. He was grinding himself into dust, and the fear-giant was constantly baking bread in the stove he called his head. The headaches had become constant, ubiquitous, all consuming. The doctors talked about migraines, cluster headaches, tension headaches; and he was prepared to believe them all, but in the end, they couldn't stop the pain, they couldn't even touch it… only junk did that, junk worked.

The saddest thing he'd ever had to admit, junk worked. But the cost… the cost that demanded it was worth the price. There was no-one to blame; he refused to dissemble. He would not be that person.

He was sick of the junky excuses, he'd heard them all, in the squats, the dealer pads, the stairwells, the therapy groups; 'it wasn't me, it was Daddy, it was Mummy, it was Uncle Bob, it was my wife, it was society, the Government, God, bad luck, fate,' - all bullshit. It was I. He had decided to take the medicine, so he was to blame. His junk, his choice, his cure, his path, his medicine. And it was killing him; of course it was killing him. It had already killed his life and now nothing but the shell of him was left. He knew it; there was nothing he could do about it; nothing he wanted to do about it. Bring it on. He just wished it would hurry up. He was tired of the weight, tired of the wait and tired of waiting with the weight. Life had become an elongated yawn; and he wanted to shut his mouth, close it off. Time gentlemen please, please, please.

Somewhere in the fog of his life they'd been a woman. He'd mistaken her fear for anger too. The shrillness in her voice had cut too deep, and her love had been so intense it was unbearable; he'd had to cut her loose. She'd tried to stay, begged him to get clean; and that had been intolerable. She had to go, and as she wouldn't, he'd left and never looked back. He didn't dare, couldn't bear to. But eventually, the face he'd run away from, faded into a shadow he'd keep hidden within himself, so deep now, not even he could find it. He told himself he'd loved her, and leaving her proved it was true love… whatever that is.

Hadn't there been a girl? Another girl at the club last night? That was it, he'd played at the Five Spot last night, or was it yesterday? Whatever, he'd played at the Five Spot, and they'd been a girl; was she still here? Billy forced his ten-tonne head to scan the room. A pair of high heels lay in the chink of light coming from the washroom. A black bra hung on the washroom door handle. He didn't wear high heels, he didn't wear a bra, never had, so who'd they belong to? The girl? The girl from the Five Spot? That would make sense. Maybe the girl was in the washroom? Maybe he should go and check, maybe he should, but he wouldn't, he knew he wouldn't. And then he saw it, a dark brown toe with bright red nail polish, sticking out from beneath the white bedsheet. It was a beautiful thing. Red as blood, crimson. It wasn't his. He didn't paint his toenails, never had… no that wasn't true, there was that one time;

just for giggles. He'd dropped in on that cat over on 6ᵗʰ Ave, the Flower District; Zoot was there playing his heart out. They blew one together for a couple of hours, and then this uptown chick, a beatnik-wannabe, started draping herself all over him… what was her name? God knows where they ended up, but he ended up with painted toes; pink if he remembered right; what was her name? Never mind, doesn't matter, it can't be her toe either, that was a long time ago, before the tide went out. Billy looked from the toe to the high heels and waited for his mind to make the inevitable connection; so that's where she was, in his bed. The girl from the Five was in his bed - cool. Billy reached out an arm that felt so far away and so heavy it could have belonged to a statue in Vermont. He watched his far away fingers take hold of the sheet and pull. The saxophone clattered to the floor, followed by the sheet. And there she was, beautiful, naked as a babe, black as a button, skin so smooth it reflected the light better than his old saxophone; beautiful. But still, very still. Billy zeroed in on her chest; not a difficult thing to do; natural even, but those stirrings were long gone; this wasn't desire this was practical; he needed to check she was breathing. He locked on - watching, watching, watching for so long, he forgot what he was watching for… breathing that was it. This junk was strong, there was no doubt about it. Clean and strong, perhaps too clean, junk like that could take you under before you knew you were sinking. The responsible thing to do would be to cut it, break its back, just to ease the trip, junk like that was too strong. His eyes focused on the curve of the girl's breasts, firm, dark breasts, full of light, but still, very still.

Billy felt his breathing beginning to get away from him. His chest felt like a red rubber ball riding a wave, bobbing up and down but always drifting away. It looked like it was coming back in on the next wave but undeniably, inextricably it was going out with the tide; being washed away. He was going under, and he really didn't mind; he knew he'd come up somewhere… and if he didn't, he didn't mind - but the girl, he minded about the girl, she wasn't used to the shit, she couldn't handle it, he had to do something. His far away, heavy hand reached for the phone beside the bed, he needed to reach it for her sake; he needed to pull her in from the tide, and if he couldn't do it, he needed to call someone who could; he needed help.

His far away fingers took hold of the receiver and tried to lift it, but it was so heavy, too heavy, why did everything have to be so heavy? There was a cat, a cat sitting on the receiver. A beautiful cat washing itself as it sat on the phone. That was cool, cats were cool, but he needed the phone, he needed to call, to get help for the girl, the girl needed help because she wasn't used to the junk and this junk was pure and strong and it was his junk, and that made her his responsibility. This was an emergency, a heavy situation and he was too far away to deal with it. He had to call someone, but the cat was on the phone. The cat was on the phone – that was almost funny; cat on a phone, who you gonna call cat? No, he needed to make a call, he needed to get help.

Billy waved his heavy far away hand at the cat. The cat just batted it away and resumed its ablutions. A hepcat for sure, crazy cat sitting on a phone. Wonder how it got there, who let it in? So tired, so tired. Time to go with the tide, go play with the undertow... beautiful tone of the... but the girl, he couldn't go with the girl on his conscience, he couldn't carry that weight out into the sea of oblivion with him, he'd drown; and what if he had to carry that weight for eternity? It was too much, too heavy man, too much, too much, too...

The man standing by the bed dressed in a trench coat and trilby hat, didn't need to show Billy his badge; Billy knew he was the man. They all looked the same. Broad shouldered heavies, with square jaws, chewing matchsticks like something from a bad movie.

'Do you know her name Billy?'

'No man, I don't know her name. Why don't you ask her?'

'Ask her? That's funny Billy. She's been dead for two days.'

'She's dead?'

'Yeah Billy, she's dead. And that's your junk in her arm right?'

Billy tried to sit up, but his back was as stiff as concrete, and his head felt like it was going to crack open, 'I tried to call man, I tried to call but there was a cat on the phone.'

'Yeah, sure there was, there always is. You're going down for this one Billy, make no mistake, you're going down.'

'That's okay with me Boss,' Billy sighed, 'I've already drowned.'

DELTA CAT

As the first light of dawn flickers across the river Omo, little Ife leaves the shelter of her grandmother's tukul and makes her way to the water's edge. Ife likes to start her day by talking to the fish, but today she has come with a song. A serious undertaking, Ife has taken upon herself after hearing her grandmother's tales of benevolent fish, that give themselves up to the villagers in times of hardship. All you have to do is treat them with kindness and respect, and sing them a song that charms their little fishy hearts. If you get it right, the fish throw themselves into the nets; and Ife wants her father's catch to be a good one today, because her grandmother is ill and needs to eat well to get better.

Ife sings her song about the loveliness of the river, and then tells the fish all about her fears for her grandmother and her family's hardship, and the great meal her mother will make of their sacrifice, and promises she will come and sing to them again if they are kind enough to help them out. And although the fish don't instantly throw themselves at her feet, she is sure the fish will see sense and come to their aid just as soon as her Papa puts his net in the water – because fish are decent creatures and care about the people who live beside the river. She then washes her face in the lapping water and heads back to the safety of the tukul.

As she approaches the cluster of huts that form her small village, she hears an unfamiliar sound coming from a tussock of grass; it sounds like a baby crying, but other, it's puzzling, intriguing. Ife checks about her, there's nobody else around to discover what it is, so she has to do it. Ife drops to her knees and crawls towards the strange cry. What she finds there is a short haired cream-coloured creature with flame speckled eyes, suckling eight mewling fist sized multi-coloured creatures. Ife's upbringing has instilled an attitude of caution towards animals within her. But this a small creature, feeding even smaller creatures…. And they look so sweet. The cream-coloured creature looks into Ife's eyes and slowly blinks; Ife returns the slow blink and sits down to take in the scene. The creature's body starts to pulse, tighten and contract, and there it was another tiny bundle of wet fur, a little grey, brown, black striped, squirming thing with tightly closed eyes. The cream-coloured creature was too tired to help its own young, and the grey thing was too weak and helpless to find its own way to its mother's teats. Ife had watched woman in the clan feed their babies, and watched the family's goat suckle its young, and once saw a giraffe suckle its baby – a ridiculous sight. She knew the grey little striped thing would die if it didn't feed. So, she reaches in, takes hold of the warm little blob, wipes the mucus from its nose and places it against its mother's teat. The blob suckles; its mother gives Ife a slow blink, and Ife again returns the signal. And then her Papa calls her from the door of the tukul, and she runs to his side.

The fishing that day was good, and Ife's grandmother ate well that night, they all did. True to her word, Ife sang a song of thanks to the fish the very next morning, and it was then she remembered to check on the cream-coloured creature and her babies. She soon found the tussock, but instead of finding the cream-coloured creature, all she found was the mewling grey striped blob. Ife picked it up and held it to her chest. It mewed, pushed its nose into her chest and began pummelling her skin. Ife understood the message, it was hungry.

Ife carried the mewling thing into the tukul, knelt beside her grandmother's cot and revealed her find; 'its hungry grandmother, what should I feed it?'

Her grandmother's waxen eyes struggled to focus in the hut's dim light, so she reaches out a trembling finger and gently palpates the ball of fluff in her granddaughter's hands; 'its got fur, try the goat.'

Ife's mother is tending to the goats, and Ife is nervous about what she will say about her newest discovery. Ife had once brought home a baby crocodile which took a bite out of Mama's finger before Papa tossed it back into the river.

'Mama…'

'What you got there Ife?'

'I don't know, but its small and hungry.'

'So, what you going to feed it Ife?'

'Grandmother says milk, because it's got fur.'

'Grandmother says, Grandmother says… well then, it won't get any with you standing over there will it child,' she pulls her daughter forward and directs her to place her hands under the goat's udders. A warm jet of milk splashes over Ife's palm and the little creature. Ife watches the bobbing head strain to reach the source; and then it's suckling.

Ife takes her little ball of fluff with her wherever she goes, at first nestled against her chest and then in a pouch her mother fashions out of a piece of worn leather, and soon the thing is no longer a helpless ball of fluff. It sits on her shoulder or chases after her heels as she goes about her chores, singing to the fish, gutting and cleaning the fish and collecting firewood. And if it ever wanders away, Ife knows just where to find it, latched onto the she-goat.

Its late one evening, and the whole family are gathered around a fire under the stars. Ife is making her grandmother laugh with her dancing, when the little grey striped thing launches itself at Ife's ankle, nearly knocking her into the fire. When the shouting and dust have settled, the creature is sitting there, holding the limp body of a black snake in its teeth.

'Tinishi Anibesa,' her grandmother declares. And from that day on, they called the little grey striped thing, Tinishi, and its place in the family is never questioned.

Collecting driftwood takes up much of Ife's day, and although her mother tells her never to venture from sight of camp, some days the river is not as generous as it could be, and she has to go a bit further than her mother's commands would allow. On this particular morning Ife strays just beyond the bend in the river, she looks back to check her position. The tukuls are hidden behind the rising sand dunes, but Ife can see the smoke rising from the campfire, so feels safe. Tinishi sits bolt upright on her shoulder playing with her braids. The sun is high in the cloudless sky, the birds are raising their squawking cries and the flies are busy being annoying. Tinishi's claws suddenly strike into Ife's shoulder. Ife lifts him down from his perch and tries to cradle him in her arms. His body is taut, his fur standing on end, and his eyes are wide open, fixed on a point in the distance. Ife looks up and freezes. A huge lion with a matted mane is charging towards her. Ife sees its teeth, its claws, and recognises death; but cannot move her feet. Ife feels the lions power swallowing her, as it gains ground with every stride; it devours her will, her strength, her life from her body, as it races towards her. She doesn't even have the strength to scream. And then, sitting on the ground at her feet is Tinishi's cream-coloured mother. The lion leaps blocking out the sky. The cream-coloured creature leaps upwards, on a collision course. Nose to nose, tooth to tooth they meet in mid-air. The sun explodes. A storm cracks the air. The earth shakes. And the lion is shredded before Ife's eyes, its fur scorched, its flesh boiled, and its bones shattered.

Ife opens her eyes to see the blue sky above her and the sun back in its place. She's laying on her back but has no memory of falling. She looks to her feet and sees Tinishi rubbing noses with his mother. The cream-coloured creature looks at Ife and gives her a slow calm blink. Far off Ife hears her mother and father calling her name. She sits up, so they can see her, and she sees that Tinishi is alone, the cream-coloured creature has gone. The ground around Ife is still smoking, blasted black by fire. She stands and feels a sharp pain in her heel, a sliver of shattered jawbone has pierced her heel. Ife sees the blood, feels the world twist, and falls. Her Papa catches her up in his arms and carries her back to the tukul.

'What happened Ife? We saw lightening, are you hurt? What happened?' her mother garbles over and over, 'what was that Ife? What happened?'

Ife doesn't have the words. Doesn't know how to explain, and feels too weak to talk, sick and aching, just as if she'd been in the sun too long. The girl can't even manage to cry. Her Papa lays her in her cot, and her mother brings her goat's milk, as her grandmother washes her body to cool her down. Ife raises no complaint although her foot throbs, and her head aches. The pain seems very far away, and the lion in her mind is getting ever closer. She sees the lion leap, hears its roar, feels its breath, and smells its burning flesh. That night, her fretting parents watch over little Ife, and Ife sleeps with terror, and sweats it through her every pore.

Ife wakes late the next morning to the sounds of the fishing boats setting out. She hasn't sung to the sea. She needs to play her part. Ife pulls herself out of the cot and sets out for the riverbank. But her feet won't walk in a straight line. The world begins to swing and then spin, and the next moment the world is upside down and Ife is lying face down in the sand.

Ife wakes up in her cot and is violently sick, her grandmother washes her down and sings her a song to get her to sleep. She wakes again, and her stomach betrays her, and her grandmother cleans her up and never says a word to shame her. They feed her herbs and milk, but Ife is sick again. At last, Ife complains that her foot is hurting, and her grandmother sees the black lines tracking up her leg from the wound in her foot; and begins to cry. In the night she hears Mama crying and wonders why? Has something happened to grandmother? Has her father been taken by the river? Ife tries to sit up to ask, but her head won't let her, and she's too tired to try again.

Ife is aware of a warm weight on her chest, and a rasping tongue licking the tip of her nose. Is the lion on her? She opens her eyes and sees Tinishi sitting on her chest. Her mother is asleep beside her. Her grandmother is snoring in her cot, and she can hear father muttering in his sleep. Her family are with her, there is no reason to be afraid. Tinishi purrs, Ife tries to pat him, but can't raise her hand. It doesn't matter, he's such a pretty thing. She's glad to have such a friend. Tinishi blinks slowly, Ife returns the gesture, Tinishi blinks slowly, and Ife closes her eyes.

He feels the girl's chest still beneath him and knows her part in his story is over. He sniffs her hair, rubs his head against hers, to fix her scent in his whiskers and presses his nose to her lips, then sits back on his haunches, and disappears in a ball of blue light.

GILES ON A HOT TIN ROOF

Giles felt like a hot ball of fuzz. Heat he could deal with, but the humidity; it was playing havoc with his fur. He'd spent the entire day resting in the shadow of an Angel Oak, but as the sun dropped and the moon took to the sky, he'd shifted his slinky self to the big house's red-tiled roof to get what little breeze there was to be had. The dry heat of the tiles felt good against his fur, but he could feel trouble's braids beckoning him; the rattle, rattle of troubles, frayed braids, how he loved their call… but it was hot, too bloody hot, tonight trouble would have to do without him.

A sleek silver car tore along the gravel driveway and screeched to a halt in front of the house. The driver's door opened, and the driver fell out. A bottle of rye whiskey in one hand and a smoke in the other. The front door slammed shut behind him. A moment of silence hung in the heat, and then the voices began.

'Where you been all day Cliff? I've been worried sick. Big Mama's been on the phone most of the afternoon.'

'What of it?'

'You've been drinking Cliff.'

'Of course I've been drinking, had to come home to you didn't I.'

'You're drunk.'

'I said I've been drinking didn't I.'

'What is the matter with you? Big Mama says you got yourself arrested…'

'That's right, that's right I did. But Big Mama saved the day again. Big Mama, Big Mama. She ain't your Mama, she's mine and I don't give a damn, what Big Mama says.'

'I can't talk to you when you're like this, go to bed.'

'You telling me what to do woman?'

'Go to bed Cliff, you're drunk.'

'I know I'm drunk. I said I'd been drinking, And I'll go to bed when I'm good and ready, not when you tell me to do nothing. You can't tell me to do nothing, this is my house you hear.'

'This is our home Cliff.'

'My house you hear, my house.'

'Well if that's the way you want it, maybe I'll go.'

'You wouldn't dare.'

'Maybe I would, maybe I'm so sick of seeing you this way Cliff that leaving would be easy. You're making it easy for me Cliff? You want me to leave is that it?'

'You can leave anytime you want Sugar, ain't no-one here stopping you. But where you gonna go that's the question? Or maybe, who you gonna go to?'

'What's that supposed to mean?'

'You think I'm blind? You think I'm stupid?'

'I think you're drunk.'

'I told you I been drinking didn't I. Now tell me where you gonna go? Who's gonna have you? Or should I say whose had you Sugar, who's been dipping his finger into my Sugar's bowl?'

'You're drunk and disgusting, I'm going to bed.'

'You'll leave when I say so bitch.'

A crash, the sound of glass smashing, followed by a scream of fear, then pleading, followed by a cry of pain.

'I told you I been drinking, why you push me Sugar, why you push me, you gotta learn Sugar, you got some learning to do.'

Weeping, agonised, disconsolate weeping. The front door swings back on its hinges. Another scream of fear, and now sobbing and pleading intermingle, and then the screaming and the sobbing is outside in the hot night air. The front door slams shut.

'No Cliff, no, please stop, stop.'

'You got it coming sugar, you got it coming.'

The car door slams, the engine revs; the woman's shrieks mix with the scream of spinning tires. The roar of an overdriven engine. Giles Bastet, 9th heavenly cat, stretches, saunters to the edge of the roof and looks down. He sees the sleek silver car spinning past a screaming woman, spitting gravel and dust at her as it eats up the driveway. A clunky ripped gear change and the car speeds backwards, taking its position at the end of the drive. The front-end of the car dips like a raging bull as the motor guns. The woman scrambles to her feet, and runs to the front door – but its locked. The car's engine strains to be released.

'No Cliff, Cliff don't.'

The gear engages the car shoots forward, second gear rams home and screams up to third.

'Cliff!'

Giles Bastet leans forward and drops. The roof of the car implodes. The driver of the car implodes, the wheels of the car spin off in four directions, the crank shaft shatters and each and every shock absorber blows, as the engine embeds itself in the gravel. A spark ignites the ruptured oil tank and what's left of the wreck explodes in a ball of flame, that sets bells ringing a mile away in the little town's fire department.

Sugar watches the flames eat up the car, and feels the heat dry the tears on her face. She hopes it takes the house with it too. Let the whole lot burn. She doesn't need any of it; she had everything she wanted, and then he drank it all away. And then… well, she must be plum crazy out of her mind, that's all there is to it! There she was watching the flames lick the sky when she saw a little tabby cat stroll right on out of those flames, as if it was strolling down the street on a Sunday afternoon. And then, well it was the darndest thing she'd ever seen, the cat climbed, no not climbed; it didn't climb at all; it just walked straight up the side of the house. Didn't even break stride, still going on its Sunday stroll, straight on up the side of the house. Craziest thing she'd ever seen. But she'd swear it was true;

but when the fire trucks turned up, bells a ringing, she forgot to mention the cat.

'You okay Sugar? What the hell happened to that car? Is that Cliff's car?'

'He was in it.'

'Jesus, get the hoses on that car! What happened Sugar?'

'Something hit the car.'

'What? A goddamned meteorite?'

It was a hot crazy night, a crazy hot terrible night, her head hurt, and she had blood in her eyes and all over her dress. Maybe Cliff's bottle of rye had dislodged more than her scalp; why would she add to the night's sad craziness with a story of a gravity defying cat? She had to work out what she was gonna tell Big Mama first… and what she was never going to tell her.

GILES & THE SCRIBES

Giles paced the linoleum floor, driven to distraction by the old woman's tuneless warbling and her inability to grasp that he wanted to be fed; now. Why was service so appalling these days? You came in, you told them what you wanted and what did they do? 'Hello kitty-kitty-kitty.' After twelve thousand years you'd have thought the humans would have grasped the fundamentals of communication, but no, still they witter on 'kitty this, kitty that;' things had really gone downhill since that milk obsessed, cheese stinky queen fell onto that viper.

'Shut up old woman and get my food!' Giles' tail declared – but did the old crone do it, no she did not.

'Are you hungry kitty?'

At last! 'No I like spending time with you ridiculous creatures, that's why I'm here,' is what Giles felt like saying, and indeed he could have said it – but the last fifty-three old women he'd spoken to had died on the spot, and he'd completely sworn-off eating old lady since living with the Tibetan hermit who ate her own frostbitten toes; nothing would persuade him to do that again.

'Here you go, hungry kitty,' a shallow plastic bowl was placed at his feet. Giles stepped forward to be greeted by a brownish mound of pungent indeterminate meaty substance, that looked as if it had been pre-chewed and regurgitated by a dog. Such an insult could not be tolerated; he was Giles Bastet, 9th Heavenly Cat, lord high overseer of accidental death, for meowing out loud!

'Is this an insult, or are you just stupid?'

The old servant nearly jumped into her sink with fright, 'oh my god.'

'That's right and don't you forget it. You don't expect me to eat that do you? I'm Giles Bastet, 9th Heavenly Cat. I've eaten warmed fat from the sacrificial altar, been offered golden dishes of human blood, flavoured with honey and Mayan chocolate; and you think I'm going to eat…that!'

'Oh me heart,' said the servant clutching her chest.

'Oh sit down before you fall down… I really can't be doing with this, I'm off,' this said, Giles Bastet, turned his puckered arse to the servant, and disappeared in a flash of blue light. Whether he heard the old dear fall to the floor and gasp her last; is conjecture I really don't feel qualified to comment on.

When your domesticated cat tires of your idiocy, it will stroll a couple of houses down, perhaps cross a street or two, until it finds a less irritating idiot to service its needs. Things aren't so different for the immortal feline; it just so happens that their streets are a little wider and deeper in time.

The cave was an odd mix of cosey, damp and airless. Below him Giles could see ten malnourished, skin clad humans, huddled around a lacklustre fire. The decor was rudimentary; stone on stone, but then again, wasn't that exactly what he needed right now, to get back to basics? He needed to figure out where and when the servants' attentiveness had drifted off their divinely appointed tasks. There had to be something he could do about the bloody awful service his mortal descendants were being subjected to; and when he found the lazy bastards responsible, he'd rip off their heads. With this objective settled in his mind, Giles settled down to wash.

Below him the gathered humans began to converse in grunts and hand signals, until one of their elders (it could have been male or female, it was difficult to tell) emitted a prolonged, low rhythmic groan. All others fell silent, as the groan dipped and rose in pitch and volume, rebounding off the cave's walls creating a chorus of faltering voices to accompany the flickering shadows that danced around their human templates. Another voice joined in the pattern, and then another and soon all the humans were groaning and rocking in unison. Giles stopped washing, mesmerised, he sat transfixed, tongue out, one leg in the air. One of the humans stood, and with muddied hands and a blackened burnt stick began creating images on the cave wall. Giles watched as a horned animal appeared, followed by three stick figures with spears: clearly humans on the hunt. Giles Bastet, 9th Heavenly Cat, nearly fell off the planet; 'So that was it…'

For millennia he'd watched priests and scribes create symbols on clay tablets, papyrus, mummified remains and temple walls, but he'd always thought their act of making was for his amusement. The scratchy, scratchy, wiggly, wiggly of the sticks and brushes were so reminiscent of a scurrying mouse; what else was he to think? But now he saw; the marks themselves meant something to the humans. The humans had a way of communicating that he hadn't grasped; could this be the key to their increasingly poor service? Was it indeed a planned subversion?

Giles dropped from his ledge, walked straight up to the wall painter, and rubbed his head against the creature's dirty shins; it was a disgusting thing to have to do, but if he was going to trace the clods vibrations across time and space, he had to get them into his whiskers, and only a head rub would do that. The servant stretched down a muddy hand to touch him, Giles spat, turned his tail on the presumptuous oaf, and walked into the fire. Once again, it is not for me to comment on the ensuing pandemonium that followed Giles' departure. I will merely report the facts; the startled artist stumbled backwards into a jagged granite vein protruding from the cave's low roof. Blinded by panic and pain the artist ran for the safety of the simple hearth. Unfortunately, the poor light emanating from the simple hearth hid a child, seeking comfort in the foetal position on the cave floor; the subsequent collision caused the frantic artist to topple headfirst into the fire. Luckily, as the fire was so feeble, and assistance close at hand; the artist was retrieved from the flames before too much damage was done. Regrettably, the ensuing screams did alert a hungry bear that had been slumbering in the dark recesses of the cave. I will leave the rest to your own internal storyboard.

Giles emerged from the fire in a small room in Italy, it felt like Verona but could have been Ravenna. It was night and a man in a white skullcap and a heavy red dressing gown, sat at a desk with a row of flickering candles before him. Giles could see the end of a goose feather quill twitching in the man's hand; the scratch, scratch, scratching it produced, was utterly bewitching. Giles could feel his fur tingle. He had to see. He shot across the room and jumped up onto the desk.

'Salve cattus,' the man with the quill laughed, 'quomodo huc venisti?' Giles knew his Latin, but he wasn't interested in conversation. His attention had been drawn to the tip of the quill; it was covered in a black fluid – and the paper over which the quill now hovered was covered in black marks. Giles leaned in to view them more closely. 'Mind the candle now you silly cattus, how did you get in here? Does my penmanship interest you cattus? Do you approve of the Italian or are you strictly a Latin cattus?' Giles couldn't make head nor tail of it; it was just rows and rows of squiggles; how could they convey meaning? 'It's a tale of one man's descent into the circles of hell. A variation of Orpheus and Eurydice…without Eurydice. It's a contemplation of fate, faith and the divine justice of God. It will never sell. It may never be read… the church will see to that.' Giles' ears twitched with excitement; here it was, proof that the servants' scribblings conveyed meaning, indeed, somehow those little squiggly lines told tales, and the tales they told were of heroes, eternity and even gods – what were the bastard servants saying about him? 'Come now cattus, time for you to go.' The man stood, crossed the room, and opened the door, 'out you go cattus, thank you for dropping by, but I have work to do.' Seeing as the servant was being so polite, and seeing as he had no wish to stay, Giles sauntered slowly out the door, nose held high, tail erect, as a passing rebuke. 'Take your time cattus, off you go. Vale cattus, vale. How did he get in here?' The man continued to chuckle as he returned to his desk. I feel it would be churlish to hold Giles responsible for the stray mosquito that was caught in the waft of the opening door. It's true the parasite laden beast would later feed upon the sleeping Italian poet, and yes, it's bite would bring about his demise before he saw the success of his masterpiece; but we can't hold Giles responsible for that; such is the nature of life, and nature is the art of God.

Giles stepped from the buzzing blue light into the balmy haze of south-eastern aspect, to find himself standing a whisker's breadth above the clear blue water of an outdoor swimming pool. Not being given to ostentatious shows of divinity Giles extended a claw and gracefully glided into the shade of the turreted building that sat at the far end of the pool.

A white-haired cat sat on the cast-iron staircase that ran up to the buildings turret. Giles greeted the cat with a slow blink. The cat, recognising Giles' divinity, and being a traditionalist, greeted him in the formal manner and returned the blink. And thus, all territorial friction was avoided. To the untrained human eye this complex and mannered greeting would have appeared as two cats on a staircase, avoiding all eye contact, as their tails lolled in the heat of the day – but that just shows you how untrained a human untrained eye can be.

A staccato tap, tap tapping, bounced down the cast-iron steps towards them catching Giles' ear; 'what is that?'

'Bastet be blessed, that's my human's story machine,' the white cat said licking its front paw. Giles spotted the cat's extra toe; an acknowledged symbol of surefooted trustworthiness within the feline world, he would pay extra attention to this cat's opinions.

'Mother Bastet be blessed, what's a story machine?'

'Oh you know these humans, they make things to do things, bikes, boats, cars and trains to travel. They even fly now… this one's got a machine that makes stories.'

'And what are these stories about?'

'Fish.'

'Why would humans want stories about fish?'

'Bastet be blessed if I know, but he sells all the stories the machine makes, lots of them. Humans must love stories about fish. I just like eating them; fish not humans.'

'Believe me, fish taste better, I'm going to see this machine for myself.'

'Bastet be blessed,' the white cat yawned as Giles stepped over him. Heading for the tap-tap-tap tapping.

At the far end of the room a heavy-set man, dressed in shorts and a baggy striped shirt stood before a high long legged wooden desk; his hands held at chest height, his fingers working at a squat black machine – tap-tap-tap tapping. Giles just had to see.

'Hello pussycat, who are you? I've not seen you around here before. Better not let Snow White catch you in here, you'll get your ears boxed. Oh, looks like you already have. Bit of a brawler are we pussy, I like that.'

What is it with these humans and their yap-yap yapping? Is it any wonder they like hanging around with dogs? The human reached out a thick finger and rubbed Giles beneath his chin. Giles' tale twitched - the apes' fate was sealed; but first, Giles had to understand the story machine. He inspected the sheet of paper that lolled from the head of the machine; it was covered in ordered lines of black shapes ... burnt wood on walls, black squiggles on paper, black lines on paper ... he'd found the connection, but had no idea what the connection signified. This was the message, but what did it report? Giles needed to grasp the meaning behind the squiggly lines; it couldn't be that hard, humans had been doing it for centuries! The human ran a finger around the base of Giles' ragged ear; Giles batted his hand away; he'd reduce the idiot to bite sized chunks for that.

'Don't like that ah, a brawler for sure. So we'll have to give you a brawler's name. Let's see, what fits? Granero? Now there was a brawler, Ordonez?' Giles' whiskers began to hum; perhaps he'd send the remains forward in time to be packaged as indeterminate cat food; 'no you're no Granero but ... wait, I have it; Giles. Your name is Giles, don't ask me why, and it's breaking the house rules but you're a Giles if I ever saw one.'

Giles Bastet, 9th Heavenly Cat, purred, the human had spoken his holy name, a name he'd never heard spoken by a human – and for that, he'd let him live. Perhaps he could use this wise servant to teach him the meaning of the words. He'd follow his timeline, back and forth, and learn everything the ape had to offer, and then rip his head off.

Every morning the man would rise, stand at his story machine, and make it go tap-tap-tap. And Giles would be there, in his past, in his future, revisiting day after day, attentive to hour after hour. The human travelled all over the world and everywhere he went he wrote, and Giles went with him. Sometimes the servant would see him, sometimes Giles kept himself hidden, but he was always there watching. It took time to learn the right words - typewriter, novelist, writer – but time is something gods can play with, a concept is easily diverted. But concepts matter to mortals, and so, Giles would watch the man weaken and then travel back to a time when he was more vital, energised and driven – but still, in whatever manifestation Giles visited him in, the man kept writing and Giles kept learning. He learnt there were many writers, many books, and so many words. He learnt that the books contained many secrets, many tales and insights into the servants' minds; which were so much darker than he could ever have guessed; they did not believe in Bastet. They were bold in their blasphemy, they believed in new gods and then abandoned their precepts and desecrated their temples, in order to believe in new gods that they too would forsake. And now they held to a version of the truth that Giles knew to be true but devoid of faith… they were apes, and the world was theirs to rule and ruin.

Giles had never attached himself to a servant in such a way or for so long before; and it took him some effort not to kill off his human before he'd completed his task. It didn't help that this particular specimen of humanity, kept putting himself in harm's way; wars, bull runs and the like; mishaps were had – a bomb blast in Northern Italy, a skylight in Paris, shooting himself in both legs during a hunting trip, and two plane crashes in Africa, fist fights, gunplay and a truly astonishing appetite for alcohol. Their partnership was a union of catastrophe, a pact with calamity; no human could hope to survive.

Giles was sitting on the table reading the newspaper the day they brought the old man home. He was befuddled and bruised, thin as a whisker, weaker than a runt kitten.

'Hello pussycat, hello pussycat. You look just like a cat I used to know… what was his name…no it's gone. It's all going…'

Giles let the old man's hand rest upon his head and felt something he had never felt before… something he had no word for … all he knew was he didn't like to see his old servant like this, something had to be done. Giles extended his claws; he'd make it quick, painless. The man's fingers looped his ragged ear; 'Giles… Giles that was it.'

Giles had never been neutered but now he knew how it felt. He couldn't do it, but something had to be done.

'You know what Giles, I think I need to keep busy… it's no good sitting here feeling sorry for myself, I need to do something, a man needs to be busy, to be in the fight. A man can be beaten but never daunted, it's not allowed, I will not allow myself to be daunted … I think I'll go clean my guns.'

Giles didn't leave but he couldn't watch

BOOKSHOP CAT

Melvin Cahill has a dream. It may not be a dream for the ages, but it's vivid and bold; for Melvin Cahill dreams of creating a community bookshop. An asylum for the abhorred and rejected, a safe place for society's pariahs, a refuge for readers that serves tea, coffee and a selection of homemade cakes at reasonable prices. A bookshop like no other, a place of healing, a place of acceptance, a bridge spanning the gap between the shunned and the world's warm embrace.

Melvin lives in a one-bedroom flat above a charity shop. The smell of stale sweat and old shoes pervades his flat and fills his unsettled dreams with the ghosts of the unwashed. But Melvin doesn't care. He has his dream to fall back on. Melvin has toiled for Her Majesty's Revenue and Customs (Business Tax - Data Quality and Governance Division) for thirty years. He's held the same position for twenty years and never had any aspirations to rise to middle management. He doesn't have the people skills or the inclination, but he does have the tenacity to diligently carry out the dry, dull, suffocating work to the satisfaction of middle management. So they leave him alone and let him get on with the dry, dull suffocating work whilst he dreams of 'Melvin's Community Bookshop.' Every spare minute and ghost haunted night Melvin inspects his envisioned stock and re-dresses his envisioned shop-front window display accordingly. He constantly walks and reviews the shop's layout and décor to ensure the comfort and wellbeing of his would-be customers. The imagined walls were once white, but he changed them to Cornish Cream to limit the glare of the strategically placed reading lamps, and the sofa in the fiction area, used to be a chaise longue, but that's now in non-fiction, and the outsized bean bags in the children's reading area have been replaced with cartoon themed scatter cushions because they're less conspicuous when replaced. The only aspect of the bookshop that is truly settled in Melvin's mind is the private reading room at the back of the store. It will only be accessible via a concealed door, disguised as a bookcase holding the modern poetry selection; no-one reads that stuff, so the door will be easily overlooked. Melvin created a five-year, monthly rotating, password log. Being privy to the password will be the only way to gain entry to the private reading room, and beyond it, the bookshop's inner sanctum. Melvin knows his people need a safe place to gather, a sanctuary and a temple in which they can express themselves freely, far from the uninformed, judgemental, persecutory eyes of the world. He will build that temple, and others will come. They will find him, and together they will have their fun. Free of shame, free of blame, free from fear of prosecution.

Giles Bastet, 9th Heavenly Cat took the high road through the High Street; by roof top, fence, tree and signage, and why not, he was in no hurry. He could be anywhere in the world in a blue flash, but this was a go-slow kind of day, a nowhere to be in a hurry day. In truth, there was nowhere Giles wanted to be, and this is where he was, some soulless concrete town… it was probably Basingstoke; and if it wasn't it might as well be. He'd spent six cat lifetimes nestling with writers, poets, and playwrights – and what a dubious lot they were! All that sighing, self-doubt, self-acclamation and weaselly neediness! You certainly couldn't judge a book by its maker, but writer's predilections for alcohol and cigarettes meant that even the briefest time in their company was sure to end badly for them, after the twelve death by burning bed, Giles kept his distance and began to frequent libraries - public and private - absorbing all the knowledge he could find. Although he'd had to flit from one library to another at a rapid rate in order to keep the librarian death toll (falling from ladder, tripping over book / falling downstairs / lift shaft / into shelving / microfiche / photocopier) to an absolute minimum; and now Giles felt tired, and just a little deflated. His insatiable curiosity had not been sated; he'd just lost his appetite.

He'd been nestling in a German library absorbing the philosophy section; a subject that fascinated and troubled Giles in equal measure. It had come as a shock to discover that many humans only believed in one god - if at all - and had done so for some time. Although opinions on who or what this god was or did, varied across time, cultures, and countries. Nobody seemed to be able to agree on this gods' actual purpose. Thankfully the old gods, wisemen, fakirs and enlightened souls of the old world were still bobbing along nicely – but he'd heard all their stories; where was the intrigue, where was the drama? This philosophy business created plenty of that; one of the philosophers even said that 'God was dead.' Others insisted gods were made in man's image and were used by rulers to control the servants and to keep them servile – a notion Giles thought was plainly ridiculous; he was a cat, not made in man's image and the servants clearly weren't servile enough. But the idea that he'd been created by mankind's need to assuage their fears caused a strange vibration in his whiskers. His brother Frank Bastet 8th Heavenly Cat, had said something about accidents happening without his influence, could it be true? The whole situation was ridiculous, he'd set out to discover why humans had become so lazy and now he was doubting his own facticity. This philosophy was dangerous stuff, it was even effecting his vocabulary.

It was a bright afternoon in May when a raucous ramble of humans stormed the library, grabbed hundreds of books – including the one's Giles was absorbing - and stormed out again. Giles was furious and more than a little intrigued; the cheek of these goons; what did they think they were doing? They didn't sign for any of the books! And taking titles from the reference section was strictly prohibited. He'd just have to do something about it; with the tingle of Heidegger in his fur Giles bounded out of the library and onto the streets of Berlin. He found a huge crowd of baying youths and uniformed men gathered around a bonfire, burning books – burning books! Burning secrets, burning knowledge, burning words written by somebody, he'd probably spent three lifetimes with; it was a furball too far. It was a level of idiocy he couldn't grasp. When did this nonsense start? Now there was a question, he had to find an answer for…

The English loved burning books, in 1812 their army murdered a whole library that didn't even belong to them! In 1915 Giles watched the official English executioner publicly kill a stack of books in the middle of London. Seventy-four years later he watched another book being crucified, doused in lighter fluid, and burnt by an angry mob who wanted to kill the man that wrote the book – inexplicably strange behaviour – if they didn't like the book, why not just leave it on the shelf? It made no sense. And it only got worse.

Seeking solace in the familiar, Giles rolled time back and flicked his claw through the years of human folly; only to discover it was always worse. Humans burnt books as a matter of course; almost as often as they wrote them. They were always at it. From the Old Emperor to the last Empire, they all burnt books, even Mother Bastet's (may she be Blessed) original servants burnt books. Giles saw the mighty library of Alexandria burn at least three times; although one account, something about a talking donkey trying to kill the Pharaoh, sounded a bit unlikely, but then again he'd read of stranger things in books - vampires, economics, psychology - but nothing, nothing as strange as the actual act of burning wisdom.

As Giles hopped from shop frontage to bus stop roof, he was convinced his quest to understand humans was doomed to failure; but it was at that exact moment that he spotted a bookshop on the other side of the street. This was a place where people who wanted books went. He dropped down onto the pavement, crossed the road at the appointed place – a practise he'd discovered in something called the Highway Code – and darted into the shop.

'Pussycat!' a young child in knee length shorts and a bright red t-shirt proclaimed.

'So it is!' the oyster skinned man behind the cash register beamed.

'Is it yours?' the child's mother asked, 'do you want me to shoo it away.'

'No, what's a bookshop without a cat? You know, I've been planning this place for years but the one thing I couldn't get sorted was a cat. Leave him, he's fine.'

'He doesn't have a collar. You'll have to give him a name,' the woman grinned as the balding man handed her a receipt

'Indeed I will, say what's your name little fella?'

'Samuel!' the child declared with a little jump.

'Then Sam it is,' the man pronounced, 'Sam the bookshop cat.'

'My hairy arse,' thought Giles.

'Thanks for coming, enjoy your book Samuel. You come back and see Sam anytime you like. You have a good day now, bye, bye. Bye, bye.'

As the little boy waved from the doorway, Melvin eyed the child's smooth calves, and brushed the perspiration from his brow.

Giles perused the shelves. What to read? He raised his tail to the fiction section, who needs fiction, the universe is perverse enough as it stands. What he needed was some facts, something solid to rest on; history? No, he'd had enough of that. The military section then, no that meant war, and he'd seen too much of that too, and wasn't war history? More philosophy then... no that crap didn't make any difference to anybody, not even the people who wrote it lived by it. What else did these scribblers have to offer? Giles regarded the cooking books but decided they would only make him hungry or turn his stomach; he needed something a bit more esoteric, something a bit more challenging. D.I.Y? Gardening? The children's section looked nice, the pillows weren't silk, but they looked comfortable. And the large mirror set in the wall was prettily painted with scantily dressed little girls with wings. But what was this hidden away at the back of the shop; Modern Poetry?

Giles had encountered a few poets in his time, the best of the lot was a loon of a lord with a clubfoot who kept a bear and a wolfdog in his house. An incredible drunk who seemed completely irresistible – and unable to resist – both men and women. He seemed to be able to write drunk, sober, naked, or mid coitus. But when it came to animals the man was a real devotee. He'd wept for days when one of his stinky dogs died, and built a monument to him too. Nobody had built a monument to Giles in a thousand years. Giles had read his stuff and liked it; so perhaps he should check out this modern lot too. Giles climbed onto the third shelf, and squeezed himself into the space between the books and the fourth shelf, and settled down to read.

Giles was just coming to terms with the nonlinear caprices of free form poetry when he heard Melvin announce the bookshop was closing, then an extraordinary thing happened; a large sweaty man in an ill-fitting raincoat walked up to the bookshelf, opened it and walked right through. And it wasn't raining outside. A few minutes later another man, a scrawny looking thing with reptile eyes walked up to the bookshelf and did exactly the same thing. When did bookshelves become doors? What on earth was going on? The chance to find out came a few minutes later when yet another desperate looking man, with questionable personal hygiene, walked up to Modern Poetry and walked right through, but this time Giles was right on his heals.

The room beyond Modern Poetry was a poky dimly lit cupboard with a sweaty redlight ambience. The walls were lined with bookshelves, except for the wall beside the door which seemed to be a smokie window with a chair set in front of it. The reptile eyed man didn't bother looking at the books but walked right up to a shelf directly opposite the window, knocked twice and said; 'Geranium.' The shelf opened and he walked through, into the darkness. Where was the other creepy looking guy in the raincoat? What was going on beyond that door?

Giles took a quick wander around the shelves and instantly wanted to cough-up a furball; this stuff was wrong, very wrong. There were no words for a start, it was all pictures, and the pictures were disgusting – beyond disgusting – disgusting and disturbing. Giles was shocked and he'd spent time looking at the walls in Pompei. Giles could feel in his tail that something very wrong was going on beyond that door and Giles was going to do something about it.

Melvin stepped through the bookshelf door, and immediately spotted Giles' presence; 'How did you get in here Sam? This is no place for you kittycat.' The insolent bald bastard stroked Giles' chin and then reached for the scruff of his neck; Giles remembered the words of Jane Austin, 'I will be calm. I will be a mistress of myself,' and allowed himself to be bested. Melvin picked Giles up and gave him a sharp shake; 'Got you now pussycat.' He knocked twice on the bookshelf and pronounced, 'Geranium;' and the bookshelf opened.

Giles was carried down a flight of metal stairs into a dank airless cellar that stank of sweat and fear. Three men were waiting at the bottom of the stairs, Mr Raincoat, Mr Reptile and a thin youth with close cropped hair and the complexion of a wet pizza. Excited smiles were plastered over their sweaty faces.

'What you got there Mel?' Pizza face panted.

'Brought a pussy to the party Mel, not your usual style,' Mr Raincoat smirked.

'What's the idea Melvin, I got allergies you know,' Mr Reptile pouted.

'You don't have to touch him Dick, I just thought it might add a little something to the party. Spice things up.'

'Really, how?' Reptile Dick sneered.

'Well... let's see.'

Giles was carried to the centre of the room and dangled over a small cage which Melvin proceeded to kick.

'Stop pretending I know you're not asleep.' A pair of terrified white eyes opened in a dark-skinned face, 'see the kitty cat? You like the kitty cat? Well, here's the thing, I'm going to let you play with the kitty cat. But first you've got to be nice to your uncles. No more biting. And if you're real nice I'll let you keep kitty. If you don't...' Melvin took hold of Giles' tail and gave it a vicious twist – Giles thrashed and writhed but was utterly powerless. 'Out you come little one, out you come. Come and play, let's have some fun.'

'Little Ife...' Giles felt the name echo through his whiskers.

The little girl climbed out of the cage, shaking from head to foot.

'Good girl. So, who's first. Me I think.' Melvin tossed Giles to one side and undid his trousers. 'Come on now, show me how much you like it. Come on now Ife'

Ife...Giles sprang in front of the child, spitting with claws bared.

'Shut up kitty!' Melvin roared landing a kick to Giles' side. Giles hit the wall, turned to face his enemy, and began to vibrate from whiskers to tail.

'Looks like you broke the cat Mel,' Mr Raincoat laughed.

'Screw the cat let's party,' Pizza face snarled.

Eight blue flashes lit up the room. Time froze. And eight cats appeared.

'Greetings Giles, lord high underachiever of whatever,' Frank, 8th heavenly cat of spite purred.

'Good to see you too Frank, lord high bucket of spit. Thanks for coming.'

'Greetings Giles, has something happened, has something gone wrong? Is it awful?' asked the twins, Esme and Ella 6th and 7th heavenly cats of fear and dread.

'What's the matter little brother, couldn't handle it all by yourself oh dear, what a shame,' meowed Claud, 5th heavenly cat of shame, 'nice to see you though, shame about the ear.'

'This better not be a waste of my time Giles, because I'm telling you now...' growled the ginger cat, Clive, 4th heavenly cat of retribution.

'Be quiet you. You leave him to me Giles,' said the white cat, Cynthia 3rd heavenly cat of revenge. 'I'll sort him out for you.'

'Why am I here! This place stinks, will somebody tell me why I'm here' seethed Brian, a fat dark tabby, 2nd heavenly cat of hate.

'Are you all done? Arthur, 1st heavenly son of Mother Bastet, lord high overseer of vengeance hissed. 'The niceties have been observed. So, let's quieten down.' Arthur curled his calico tail around his paws and addressed his youngest brother with a long slow blink. 'I hope you've gathered the family for a good reason Giles, we've all got busy lives you know. So why are we here?'

'The child,' Cynthia replied, 'he called for the child.'

'One human child Giles, really?' Brian growled, 'you've gathered Mother Bastet's Holy Nine, for a child.'

Giles climbed on the shoulder of the time frozen child, and rubbed his nose against her braids, 'Her name is Ife… and her memory is in my whiskers.'

'Giles, you're so sentimental,' his eldest brother chided.

'No one forgets their first,' the twins intoned.

'What would Mother do?' Cynthia sighed.

'Of course… Giles, would you be so kind as to make the request in the formal manner. I think it's what Mother would have wanted.'

Giles Bastet, 9th Heavenly Cat, lord high overseer of accidental death, wrapped his tail around the girl's neck and purred, 'I call on my brothers and sisters, Mother Bastet's Holy Nine, to defend this child.'

Arthur lifted his front paw to his nose, and extended his diamond claws, 'In that case Giles, happy to oblige.'

Time flowed; 'What the fuck is…'

Arthur launched himself into Melvin's face, fixed his claws into his bald scalp and sank his teeth into his bulbous nose. Brian landed on Melvins chest knocking him to the ground, as Cynthia tore at his exposed genitals.

Mr Raincoat screamed, rushed to Melvin's aid and was immediately torn in half by the twins.

Reptile Dick and Pizza Face made for the stairs. In a blue flash, Giles blocked their path and racked his claws across Dick's reptile eyes. Dick fell backwards, knocking the Pizza Face to the floor. Claud fell on his neck, and tore out his windpipe, sending a jet of blood across the room. Half blinded by his own blood, Reptile Dick tried for the stairs again. Frank sank his teeth into his ear, as the other cats pounced. They dragged him to the floor and tore him apart.

The only sound in the room was Ife's whimpering.

'What are we going to do with her?' Claud the tortoiseshell cat asked.

'I'll take her somewhere safe. I know good people.' Cynthia replied.

'Good people, where did you find them?' Frank sniggered.

'Never you mind…' Cynthia pushed her head into Ife's lap and they both disappeared in a blue flash.

'Job done then… I'm hungry. Time to go. So long little brother,' Brian yawned and departed.

'Thank you, Arthur, Claud, Esme, Ella and… even you Frank.'

'Even me… not that he holds a grudge or anything. Take care Giles, hope you find a cure for those fleas soon,' Frank sniped and was gone.

'It could have been worse,' the twins intoned and disappeared in a single flash.

'Shame, I was just getting going,' Claud sighed, and was gone.

Giles looked to Arthur and with a bowed head asked; 'why are the servants so… terrible.'

'It has always been so Giles. We are our nature, it's the same for them. You can't blame a tree for being a tree, you can only watch it grow and hope it bears fruit. One day it will fall over. And they always do. Take care Giles, get some rest, you look worn out.'

Giles was alone. Was it really that simple? People are people, it seemed a poor answer to all the pain he'd witnessed. And what did it mean to bear fruit? That they did this to themselves? So, what need did they have of gods? What need of him? Was that why they showed no respect because they didn't need him? Giles knew an uncomfortable answer was not necessarily a right answer, but then again, all things being in the hands of the gods, hadn't done the world any favours. Perhaps it was time to let them get on with it and make their own mistakes. Time to let them grow up. Giles' heart sank. Philosophising was so very tiring. His brother was right, he needed to rest. Giles took himself back to the bookshop and considered, where would be a suitable place to take a nap? The evening light was streaming through the window, making the spines of the books shimmer. He needed somewhere warm, somewhere he could watch human life come and go without interacting with it. Giles hopped into the shop's window display, and saw the streetlights turn on. He had to admit, here was a beauty to it, this human world, all they really needed was a break from his influence, a chance to right their own mistakes. Giles yawned; curled himself into a ball, tucked his tail under his nose, fixed his thoughts firmly on a little girl with braided hair, who once carried him beside a river in Africa. And went to sleep.

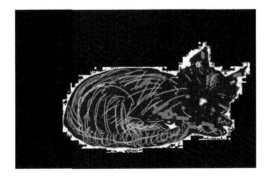

Neil S. Reddy

Lecturer & Honorary Reader in Celtic Ghost Cats at the University of Submersible South Holland & Thyme. A leading authority on Pre-Beardsley Feline Fiction and other less sticky substances, he is also known as a conduit for 18th century pre-decimal string. He also writes incredibly serious works of fiction.

Helen Lindley

Helen Lindley has been writing poetry and making up tunes since she was young. After discovering folk music, she realised she could combine the two and has developed a passion for rescuing old folk songs, that have lost their original tunes, and need deserve new ones. She sings, plays fiddle, wishes she was better at concertina, and is quite easy to spot at folk gigs, due to wearing colourful Dr. Martens boots. She lives in Lincolnshire with her husband (with whom she owns an art and woodwork business), their two children and a lazy black cat.

Tim Youster

Tim Youster was born and raised in the dry middle lands, but now lives on the wet coastal fringes. He'll happily take a stab at designing anything from your book covers to pantomime promos, the weirder the better. When he's left to his own devices he's been known to make weird photo portraits, odd pictures of Mr Toad and exciting illustrations of GIANT FIGHTY ROBOTS! He's a dog person, but has a cat and some fish. So that didn't go according to plan.

Printed in Great Britain
by Amazon

37810628R00111